"This clever novel and its smart, endearing cast of characters will have readers enchanted and eager for the implied sequel(s)."

"Gilly's plucky spirit and determination to oust the culprit will make *Flunked* a popular choice for tweens."

"There's much to amuse and entertain fans of classic tales with a twist."

"New readers will be caught up within the first few pages. Tweens who are fans of fractured fairy tales like the Whatever After series by Sarah Mlynowski (Scholastic) will have no problem getting into this read."

"Gillian remains an appealing, vibrant character, whose first-person narrative, with humorous, dramatic, and self-reflective touches, makes for fast-paced, entertaining reading."

"Mermaids, fairies, trolls, and princesses abound in this creative mash-up of the Grimms' most famous characters. This whimsical tale is a surprising mixture of fable, fantasy, and true coming-of-age novel."

—*Kirkus Reviews* on *Tricked*

"An entertaining and often humorous fantasy flight. Recommended for fans of Soman Chainani, Shannon Hale, and Shannon Messenger."

—*School Library Journal* on *Tricked*

"This fast-paced mash-up of fairy tales successfully tackles real-life issues such as prejudice, gender-role conformity, and self-esteem."

—*Kirkus Reviews* on *Switched*

"This entertaining series will satiate readers for whom Disney's *Descendants* is a year or two out of reach."

—*School Library Journal* on *Switched*

Also by Jen Calonita

Fairy Tale Reform School

Flunked

Charmed

Tricked

Switched

Royal Academy Rebels

Misfits

FAIRY TALE
REFORM SCHOOL

WISHED

Jen Calonita

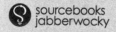

Published by Sourcebooks Jabberwocky, an imprint of Sourcebooks, Inc.
P.O. Box 4410, Naperville, Illinois 60567-4410
(630) 961-3900
Fax: (630) 961-2168
sourcebooks.com

Library of Congress Cataloging-in-Publication Data

Names: Calonita, Jen, author.
Title: Wished / Jen Calonita.
Description: Naperville, Illinois : Sourcebooks Jabberwocky, [2019] | Series: Fairy Tale
    Reform School ; #5 | Summary: Maxine, with the help of an over-enthusiastic genie,
    makes a wish that has everyone at the Fairy Tale Reform School focusing on
    producing a musical rather than figuring out how to combat Rumpelstiltskin.
Identifiers: LCCN 2018040407 | (hardcover : alk. paper)
Subjects: | CYAC: Fairy tales--Fiction. | Characters in literature--Fiction. | Genies--Fiction. |
    Musicals--Fiction. | Theater--Fiction. | Reformatories--Fiction. | Schools--Fiction.
Classification: LCC PZ7.C1364 Wk 2019 | DDC [Fic]--dc23
LC record available at https://lccn.loc.gov/2018040407

Source of Production: Worzalla, Stevens Point, Wisconsin, United States
Date of Production: January 2019
Run Number: 5013957

Printed and bound in the United States of America.
WOZ 10 9 8 7 6 5 4 3 2 1

For Katherine Prosswimmer, my partner in crime.

Be careful what you wish for...

Happily Ever After Scrolls
Brought to you by FairyWeb—
Enchantasia's Number One News Source!

Enchantasia on High Alert

by Coco Collette

Hold on to your wands and take a deep breath. At a recent village meeting, the royal court admitted an attack on Enchantasia could be imminent.

"We regret to inform you that Rumpelstiltskin is now in possession of Alva's statue," announced Princess Rose, in her first public appearance in months. "If he finds a way to free her from her cement bonds, we fear these two villains will be unstoppable." (While this news is upsetting, this reporter must note the former Sleeping Beauty looked great and revealed her "curse has been lifted.")

The announcement sent those in attendance into a panic, but Princess Ella was quick to offer some assurances.

"We don't know what Rumpelstiltskin has planned, but we are doing everything we can to protect our kingdom."

The royal court wouldn't say what measures they're taking to ensure their citizens' safety, but Princess Snow said the Dwarf Police Squad has been meeting with the royal court daily to discuss security upgrades and leads.

"Our forces are patrolling the countryside for any sign of Rumpelstiltskin and his squad," said Princess Snow. "Police Chief Pete wants us to remind you: If you see something amiss in your fairy garden or vegetable patch, say something. We will follow up on all leads." Many citizens are already flocking to Red's Ready-for-Anything Shoppe to purchase cloaking devices, powerful wands, and disappearing doors to protect their families.

"We encourage you to be cautious, but don't let your fears control you," added Princess Ella. "Go about your day and trust that the royal court will keep you well informed." Despite her assurances, many in attendance still worried about the royal court's effectiveness in protecting the students at Fairy Tale Reform School.

The school has been attacked by Alva and Rumpelstiltskin in the past, and both villains have lured students away to join their cause. "Don't worry," Rapunzel told the group. "Fairy Tale Reform School is being well taken care of."

Stay tuned for details on an imminent attack by Rumpelstiltskin and Alva!

CHAPTER 1

Ready for Anything

"Attack!"

The battle cry comes from Rapunzel as she races out of Fairy Tale Reform School with dozens of students on her heels. Every one of them has their training wand aimed and ready to strike if necessary.

Normally, we can only use our training wands in Wanding 101 or Intermediate Wanding, but as Headmistress Flora says, "Desperate times call for desperate measures."

"To the fields beyond the corn maze!" Rapunzel instructs. "Any moment they'll be upon us!"

Students stream out of the building with crossbows, bows and arrows, and slingshots. Others hold burlap bags containing potions and spell books or take to the sky on magic carpets and Pegasi. I blink rapidly when I spot a few daring kids even traveling by bubble. Professor Harlow whipped them up in her lab last week and showed them to us during a school security briefing—we have those weekly now—but the one she tested on Porter Millicent popped when he was only a few feet off the ground. I know she made modifications, but I think I'll take my chances by foot.

Zoom!

I duck as a spell shoots right over my head.

"Sorry!" Maxine calls, lumbering toward me. "Are you all right?"

The bush behind me has caught fire. I grab a pitcher of water from a nearby wishing well (*Please. What a crock!*) and pour it on the bush. No wishes granted, but the fire is out.

Maxine wipes the drool from her mouth. "I misfired again because the wand is too small for my fingers." She shows me her ogre hands, which are twice the size of mine. "Why do we have to use these things?"

"You don't." I pull an arrow from my pack. I set it up in the bow, pull back the string, and aim at the woods way off in the distance. They'll be coming from that way. I let go of the quiver and *whoosh*! My arrow lights on fire, raining sparks as it flies through the air toward its final destination. *Brilliant.*

"Wow," Maxine marvels, her right eye rolling in its socket.

"Don't give Gilly credit for that move." Jocelyn saunters over with two fireballs whirring in her outstretched hands. "It was my idea." She throws one of the fireballs into the air, and it travels for miles before landing in the trees a ways off. "That should slow them down."

Maxine frowns. "You're using an awful lot of magic lately."

Jocelyn narrows her dark eyes. Sometimes she looks so much like her big sister, Harlow (a.k.a. the Evil Queen), it's uncanny—the creamy-white skin, jet-black hair, and permanent sinister smile…or scowl.

"So what?" Jocelyn smarts. "Harlow and Headmistress Flora say it's allowed because we're at war. You'd be smart to learn some spells yourself, Maxine." She points her finger at Maxine's wand, mumbles a few words, and the wand begins to glow. "There. At least now you can disarm those scummy squad members if they come your way. One wave and you'll send them flying a hundred feet." She laughs wickedly.

"*Aaaooooh!*"

The beastly cry makes even the bravest kid stop for a

second and look around. My friends and I turn to the open castle doors and watch as a wolf in a purple party dress runs past us on all fours.

"Good girl, AG!" says Ollie, patting our friend on the back as she snuffles the wiry vegetable plants and eats a tomato from the vine. "Sniff out those evil candy-loving thugs and their friends. Which way did they go, girl?" he asks in a baby voice. "Which way?"

"Ollie, show some respect," I snap. "She's royalty." She's also the daughter of Prince Sebastian (a.k.a. the Beast, a.k.a. our professor) and Beauty (our magical librarian). Even in her beastly state, they'd be horrified if they learned Ollie was talking to her like she was a dog.

"A princess with a great sense of smell," Ollie says and winks at me. He's dressed for battle in his favorite blue velvet pirate coat he claims was a gift from a pirate on the island of Camazoo, and his dark hair is covered with a black skull-and-crossbones bandanna. Under his eyes, he has blue and black paint swiped across his brown skin. Ollie says even during war, it's important the other side knows who they're fighting (which is why he wears the Fairy Tale Reform School colors even when he's not in uniform).

"Okay, mate, go terrorize that evil troll and his friends!" He holds out an ivory handkerchief with the initials *RS* stitched into it in front of AG's...er...snout. "This was his. Get a good whiff." AG howls again and sprints away.

"Where'd you get that?" asks Jax, walking up behind us with a large scroll, a map, and a quill. It was seven in the morning when we found out we were under attack, but somehow his uniform is neatly pressed and his sash is in place. I don't know how he always manages to look like a prince even when he has no warning. My uniform is buttoned wrong and I didn't have time to comb my hair, but I did grab my bow and arrow, so there!

Ollie grins. "Swiped it from Rumpelstiltskin one time when we were in his office." He waves it in the air, and it comes this close to being taken out by a rogue spell. "Always knew it would come in handy!"

We really should find cover.

"Excellent. I'll need that when you're done today." Jax writes something on his scroll, and we all look at each other. Even Maxine rolls her eyes.

Flora, Harlow, and Rapunzel named Jax as Student Director of Battle Affairs, and well, the newfound power has made his head become as inflated as Humpty Dumpty.

He looks up at us, and we look away.

"I've got all the students accounted for and at their checkpoints except you guys." Jocelyn growls, and I squeeze her hand. "But I don't see Jack." He looks around, his blond hair turning almost white in the rising sun. "Where are Jack and Erp? How does one lose a giant?"

Thump. Thump. Thump.

The ground beneath our feet begins to shake, and Ollie and I hold onto one another to keep from toppling headfirst into the vegetable patch. A large shadow suddenly blocks out the sun, and we all look up. A giant with a boy with dark skin sitting on his shoulders is standing over us.

"Hey, Director!" Jack yells down from several stories up. "Looking for us?"

Erp, who is taller than the trees and is wearing overalls, grunts hello. He's holding onto one of the castle's conical turrets for balance. A few bricks break free and begin tumbling toward us. We all jump to get out of the way.

Jax grabs his bullhorn and shouts up to Jack, "You know this is too close to the castle for Erp. You're supposed to be patrolling the Hollow Woods borders."

Jack salutes him, and I see Jax grimace. Those two have

never really gotten along. "Aye, aye, Captain! Unless, of course, you want me to throw down a magic bean and make things in this battle really interesting."

"No!" we all shout.

The sound of cannon fire interrupts further arguing. Blackbeard and Madame Cleo are directing the battle from the water. On the great lawn, students run in various directions, getting into attack position. My friends and I really need to get moving.

Headmistress Flora's voice comes over Miri the Magic Mirror's magical loudspeaker system as if she knew exactly what I was thinking. "They've broken through the barrier! Be ready! Be ready!"

There is a sudden pop and a bang, followed by a *whoosh*. Several figures have emerged from the woods and are racing toward the school by foot and air. Rumpelstiltskin flies by us, cackling on the edge of his cooking pot ladle.

I feel my blood boil at the sight of him.

Jocelyn grabs my hand. "Come on! We're nowhere near the meeting point."

"We're going to be late for Kayla!" Ollie yells, picking up speed and running ahead of us. "If we miss our entrance…"

Boom!

A group of kids in a flying Dutch oven land in front of us and run in our direction.

"Too late!" Jocelyn begins casting spells as Rumpelstiltskin's group of loyal servants—who are mostly kids—comes rushing at us. I pull out my bow and arrow and start aiming. The arrows hit kid after kid, each one going down hard. Good!

(Okay, so I'm not actually hurting them. The fire in the arrows only stuns, so they'll lay there, unable to move, until one of the FTRS kids drags them off to the dungeon. Then we can interrogate them. I love that part.)

It feels good to hit Stiltskin's evil little cronies. I spot Hansel and Gretel coming toward me, their faces filled with hate. I fire once! Twice! And *boom*! They're facedown in the grass.

"Okay, Gilly, don't waste all your ammo," Ollie says worriedly as he uses a cloaking potion to sneak up on unsuspecting Stiltskin Squad members.

"I don't have time to make you another batch of arrows this week," Jocelyn adds as she sets the cooking pot aflame so the squad can't get back in it. "You don't need to hit every one of these kids. Remember the goal!"

Get to Stiltskin. Find Alva. Stop them both.

The words have been drilled in my head over and over, and yet, I find my eyes wandering, looking. For her.

Finally, she appears like a mirage, rushing through the smoky field as the battle rages around her. My younger sister Anna, with her long brown hair and that smug smile she adopted once she started hanging out with him, is running straight for me. And for a moment, I falter, like I have too many times before. I want to believe the best in my kid sister, but she proved in Cloud City that she cannot be trusted.

My sister is a villain.

And I am not.

The two of us head for each other. She aims her wand at me, and I raise my arrow, trying to keep the bow straight as I load up and prepare to launch.

But behind Anna, something catches my eye.

Pop! Pop! Pop! A group of kids magically appear on the grassy knoll. They must have used fairy magic to shrink themselves. The kids race toward the Stiltskin Squad members with a look of fire and fury on their faces. I have no clue who they are. They're not wearing FTRS uniforms or gold Stiltskin Squad buttons. Instead, they're wearing black capes and brandishing swords. A goblin goes tearing after Anna, and my jaw drops.

"Tessa? Is that you?" I say in surprise. "You're not wearing...pink."

As I'm looking at Tessa, Anna plows into my side, sending my bow and arrow pack flying.

"Gilly!" my former roommate, Kayla, cries, her fairy wings fluttering as she runs in my direction. "Watch out!" A squad member shoots up at her, and she flies off, out of the line of fire.

I hit the dirt, but quickly scramble to my feet and come face-to-face with Anna. My heart is pumping hard as I stare at her. We both know what we have to do, and yet, I hesitate for the slightest of moments. A second later, we're rolling on the ground, fighting like we once did back home in our boot, and all I can think is *she betrayed me.* I can't let her win. Not this time.

Flip! I have Anna on her back and her hands pinned to her side.

"Finish her!" Jocelyn shouts. "Spell her! She deserves it!"

I can hear others egging me on as my sister squirms beneath my hold. I could stun her and take her to the dungeon to be interrogated. I'd have to do it by spell since I lost my arrows. Or I could physically haul her off to the dungeon, but I might get ambushed. What to do? Before I can decide, Anna pulls out of my grasp and flips me over.

"I'm not as weak as you!" Anna shouts. "You're done for." She starts mumbling, and I realize she's probably trying to banish me somewhere like Cloud City or worse. I'm so surprised, I can't move.

Maxine comes rushing over, barreling into the two of us, sending Anna flying. "Noooo!" Maxine shouts, her voice so loud, everyone stops to look. "Goldilocks! Goldilocks! Goldilocks!"

The sounds of the battle stop. All over the battlefield, Stiltskin Squad members dissolve into thin air. When the smoke clears, Rumpelstiltskin and his cooking ladle are gone. So is Anna.

"Maxine!" I groan, lying on my back in defeat as Jax and the others gather around. "What did you do that for?"

Maxine's cheeks grow pink. "I'm sorry! I couldn't watch you fight Anna, even if she wasn't the *real* Anna. You'd never forgive yourself if you hurt her." She pauses. "And if she hurt you, you'd be upset too, and…"

"It was an apparition, you fool! This is just a practice battle!" Jocelyn shouts.

"I know, but I…" Maxine starts to sniffle then begins bawling.

"I had an hour's worth of battle plans ready to instruct!" Jax throws a scroll into the air and lets it fall in the mud.

Ollie gives me a hand up. "This is not going to be pretty," he whispers.

"And you!" Jocelyn points to me. "You had Anna, and then you got careless and let her pin you. Your sister is not going to go easy on you when she gets the chance!"

"I know!" I shout, but I have a feeling I'm shaking. "I had it under control."

"Didn't look like you did," Jocelyn counters.

The two of us start bickering as Maxine cries harder. Kayla is trying to calm everyone down while Jack, Ollie, and Jax talk over one another. Our argument is quickly drowned out by an earth-shattering scream. We all look up. Harlow is moving swiftly toward us, her purple, glittery cape billowing out behind her in the wind. Rapunzel is on her right and Headmistress Flora (the former Wicked Stepmother) is on her left. Neither look happy. This is not a good sign.

"Who foolishly shut down my battle simulation charm—which, I might add, took me a week to plan—before I was ready to end it?" Harlow asks.

We all look at Maxine. She slowly raises her hand. "Guilty as charged."

Pegasus Postal Service

Flying Letters Since the Troll War!

FROM: Mother and Father (2 Boot Way)

TO: Gillian Cobbler (Fairy Tale Reform School)

Gillian,

Father just came from the royal court meeting about Rumpelstiltskin and Alva. We think you should come home immediately.

Considering what you told us about your poor sister Anna falling victim to Rumpelstiltskin's charms, we fear he may come for our family. Father thinks he could use you or your siblings as leverage to try to get us on his side. Father is thinking of packing us all up and sending us to his mother's for safekeeping.

I know what you're thinking: Father has forbidden us

---

from letting you have contact with your grandmother, but desperate times call for desperate measures. No one knows we're even related to her, so Rumpelstiltskin wouldn't be able to find us there. Despite your father's worries, I've always thought you and your grandmother would get along well if given the chance to meet. I only met her a few times, but you remind me of her.

Consider coming home, darling. Be safe! Oh, and destroy this message after reading it!

Love,
Mother

CHAPTER 2

Come On, Get Happy

Nice going, Maxine!" grumbles a goblin boy struggling to carry a heavy box of cannon powder down the hall. "Now I have to go to the Witches in Disguise: How to Recognize Your Enemies lecture. I heard it's four hours long!"

"Sorry!" Maxine says for the umpteenth time. We are heading back to our dorm rooms to clean up. I guess she can feel us looking at her again because she turns our way and frowns. "I got scared, okay? I thought Gilly was going to get hurt."

That's not possible. Flora added the code word after Rapunzel and Harlow's first battle drill ended with an ogre smashing a month's supply of fruit and vegetables to smithereens because he suspected the harpy he encountered in the pantry closet was the real deal. (We're still eating apple-turnip mush for supper every night. Yuck.) There was recently a harpy attack at Royal Academy so I get the kid's confusion, but fairy be, there are posters everywhere.

"But you know she can't!" Jocelyn is growing impatient. "It's a drill! We have them every week! There are posters telling people *about* the drills so there's no confusion!"

She points to the castle wall that just appeared in front of us, causing us to take a left turn instead of going straight. On it is a scroll with pictures of various weapons, spells, casting books, and an ominous shadow that looks a lot like Rumpelstiltskin.

DON'T BE GRIMM—BE PREPARED FOR BATTLE!

Drills held weekly. All illusions are interactive, but unable to harm you! However, in the event of an emergency, yell *Goldilocks*,

and the battle will stop immediately.*

*Students who end Professor Harlow's simulation do so at their own risk.

Jax balances his battle plans and maps in his arms. "They really need to take the asterisk off that sign."

"But Gilly looked so unhappy!" Maxine tries again. "When Anna appeared, I…"

"I'm fine!" I snap a little too quickly, and everyone in the hallway looks at me. I take a deep breath and turn to Maxine. "I know you were just trying to help me. That's what friends do."

Maxine sniffles. "Thanks. You're such a good friend, Gilly. I…"

"Even though, you knew it was just an illusion," I can't help adding.

"A scary illusion!" Maxine continues with a shudder. "Everyone is so doom and gloom. All we talk about are attacks, and weapons, and poison apples. Can't we have fun anymore?"

Kayla snorts. "Fun? You want to talk about having no

fun? How would you like to live with a mother who has to lock herself away all day and all night, waiting for information about Rumpelstiltskin's story to come to her?" Her wings pop out and flutter before disappearing again. (They get wonky when she gets upset.) "I finally get my mother back, and now she has no time for me! It's all about that book!"

"Well, that book is important," Jax reminds Kayla. "If we have any hope of stopping him, we want to know what he's planning for Enchantasia."

"Not going to happen," Jocelyn says in that cheery manner of hers. "One villain with magic is bad enough. Two is impossible. The kingdom is done for. That's why my sister is leading battle drills. Best we can hope for is some of us make it out of here alive without getting our houses blown down."

A sprite flying next to us bursts into tears and flies away.

"Jocelyn, stop it!" Maxine chides. "You're scaring them." She calls after the sprites, "Don't worry! We're safe at FTRS! Everything is going to be fine!"

"Liar," Jocelyn mumbles. "We're doomed."

Maxine turns purple, looking angrier than I've ever seen her. She waves one of her huge hands in the air. "I'm not lying! No one knows what's going to happen next! All we can control is today, so why not be happy and enjoy yourself while you can?"

"Here comes the speech," Ollie whispers, and I bite my lip.

Bless Maxine's heart. She wants everyone to be happy, but it's tough. I want to say *Look around! We're a kingdom under attack. No one's happy.*

A new hallway opens, and I can see the circular staircases leading to the boys' and girls' dormitories right ahead of us. Students covered in mud wearily stumble up the steps to change uniforms, but Maxine blocks our path.

"When I was a wee ogress, we were in the height of the Troll War," she tells us. "Our home in the hillside was destroyed in an attack, our extended family scattered, and Father had to go off to fight. It was just me and Mother." She looks off in the distance, drool dripping down her chin. "I was so sad, but then Mother took me to a meadow to pick some flowers, and we made a bouquet to put in our new home. Sure, it was the underside of a bridge, but she tried to make it feel special. When it was safe to go outside, she'd take me to a lagoon to hear mermaids sing, or we'd hike to Mount Olimundo to have berries that we would whip into the best dessert around. Sometimes we'd even go hunting for typhiras during a summer thunderstorm."

"You went *looking* for a typhira?" I snort. "They're not real, Maxine."

"What's a typhira?" asks Kayla.

I shudder. "Supposedly they're nasty little things that hate school kids and love to cause mischief…but they're just a legend."

"They are real!" Maxine insists. "Father saw one once. He said it was kind of cute." She grins. "He said they're unique looking, like me!"

"Cute? They practically took down one of the ships I was on by making one of their freak thunderstorms," Ollie says.

"You saw one?" Maxine sounds more excited than alarmed. She turns to Kayla. "They can make storms with their minds!"

Jocelyn sighs. "Maxine, you're dreaming. Even the most powerful witch has a tough time conjuring up a storm with her mind."

"The typhiras can do it!" Ollie insists and his cheeks flush. "I mean, you wouldn't want them to make a storm on purpose. Ours happened by accident. We had one unknowingly locked up in one of the trunks I plundered from a village. You know, back when I did that sort of thing. When we let it out on the ship, it went out of control and conjured up this huge storm. I thought the lightning was going to crack our mast in half!"

"So where is this mythical creature now?" Jax says with a smirk.

"It got blown off the ship in the wind it created," Ollie says with a shrug. "And the storm died down."

"How convenient," I say under my breath.

Maxine sighs. "You're so lucky. I've always wanted to see one make a storm. But we never found a typhira. Even so, Mother and I had grand adventures, and soon I was happy again. I missed Father, our home, and our friends, but Mother kept me distracted, and suddenly the war didn't feel so close to home anymore. I remember I asked Mother why she did this, and she said, 'Maxine, the world can be a scary place, but we're okay and we need to celebrate that. No good comes from crying all the time. The more good you put out in the kingdom, the more good comes back to you.'"

"Someone get me a violin," Jocelyn says. "Next you're going to say, 'Love conquers all.'"

"Love does conquer all!" Maxine insists.

"Not always," I remind her, thinking of Anna.

"Yes, but…" Maxine starts to say, and Jocelyn shushes us.

"Do you guys hear talking?" Jocelyn snakes away from us and moves to a hallway that opened up behind the dormitory staircases. "I think that's my sister talking."

"Aren't they getting ready to teach class?" I ask. "Professor Sebastian said something about a final review for tomorrow's test."

"Ugh! I haven't even started studying," Jax says, and I look at him in surprise. "I was working on maps for the next battle drill."

"Shh!" Jocelyn shushes us again. "Listen!"

We hurry after Jocelyn. Harlow, Flora, Rapunzel, Professor Wolfington, and Blackbeard (who is carrying a mirror with Madame Cleo's image on it) are hurrying into Madame Cleo's detention room. The door shuts behind them with a click.

Miri's voice comes over the magical loudspeaker system. "Reminder! Class will resume in five minutes. All teachers are in their rooms waiting for you, which means if you're not already seated, you're going to be late!"

"Get your story straight, Miri," Ollie jokes. "These teachers aren't ready for class."

Kayla flutters to the door of Professor Wolfington's

classroom and gasps. "Guys, look! Wolfington is in there! Didn't we just see him go into the detention room?"

We rush over to the doorway and peek in. There is Professor Wolfington, in all his hairy glory, standing at the magical chalkboard pointing to information about a quiz they're having that week in History of Enchantasia. He says something about which pages to study in our course books, and we duck back out. Hans Christian Anderson, what is going on?

"That's not him," Jocelyn says. "Watch his feet. He's a hologram. It's one of my sister's favorite bait-and-switch tricks. Projecting herself elsewhere so no one can know what she's really up to." She rolls her dark eyes as she pushes her long, black tresses behind her ears. "I've gotten pretty good at it myself, but she caught me sneaking into her potion lab the other night when I was supposed to be in bed. I was trying to pinch a tiny bit of rhubarb gingersnap for this face cream I want to make, but she said no. She's so stingy."

"Could she project that many teachers into their classrooms?" Ollie asks. Jocelyn shrugs. "That is impressive. If I could do that, I would never have to go to potion lab with her again!"

"Harlow must have a really good reason to call a meeting,"

I point out. Jocelyn and I look at each other. Oh, this is too juicy to ignore. As the hallway begins to shimmer and fade away, the two of us dive into it. Maxine begins to protest, but soon follows with Jax, Ollie, and Kayla.

"I don't know if this is a good idea," Maxine says worriedly. "Last time I was stuck in there, Rumpelstiltskin tried to drown us in Madame Cleo's tank. I've avoided detention ever since."

"You're not in detention now, silly," I remind her. "We're spying. You'll be fine." Maxine doesn't look convinced.

Ollie places his eye over the keyhole. "Oh yeah, the whole teaching staff is here. And the royal court is here too. Even… wait a minute, is that Princess Rose?"

"Let me see!" I push Ollie out of the way to get a better look. The others are also jockeying for position.

It *is* Rose! She's standing next to Princess Ella, listening to something Headmistress Flora is saying with large hand movements. I need to get in there.

"How are we going to get past them?" Jax asks. "They're right by the door."

Jocelyn has her ear up to the wood. "I can't hear a blasted thing. It will take way too long to come up with some sort of cloaking spell."

"Or a diversion," Ollie says. "I mean, we could blow up the door with a spell, but then they'd all run out and that would defeat the purpose."

"Guys?" Kayla tries.

"What if it was just a teensy explosion?" I suggest. "Or we knocked and ran so they had to open the door?"

Ollie scratches his chin. "I like that. Or I could go back and get my bag of magic tricks and create my own illusion of a sea serpent busting through Madame Cleo's tank and then…"

"Guys!" Kayla points to the door. "They've moved. You don't have to blow up the door. We can just…" She picks the lock with a tiny pin from one of the green crystals woven into her hair. "…walk in." The door clicks.

"Nice move," Jocelyn says appraisingly.

"Once we're inside, we have to be really quiet and find somewhere to hide so they won't see us," Jax reminds us. "Somewhere near the door."

"The wood cubbies!" Jocelyn suggests. "We should be able to fit inside them. Kayla just has to tuck in her wings, and Maxine needs to make sure she runs to the ogre-sized one."

"I still think we shouldn't be snooping around," Maxine says. "If the professors think there's something we need to know, they'll tell us." She brightens. "Hey, maybe they're planning a party! We haven't had one in so long. It would really lift everyone's spirits."

"They're not planning a party," Jocelyn says dryly. "Now come on!" She slowly turns the door handle then slips inside. One by one, we silently follow, staring at the large tank of water in front of us. Madame Cleo resides primarily in a large fish tank in Fairy Tale Reform School, but on occasion she goes out. The tank has tunnels that connect to the nearby lake (where Blackbeard's ship is anchored) and the river that leads to the sea. Lately, she's been here, giving a lot of detention to students who aren't following safety protocols in the wake of Alva's statue being stolen. Right now, the room is empty. They must have moved into her private quarters, which are in another tank behind this one so we've got the room to ourselves. This is perfect!

The tank glimmers in front of me, full of silvery fish water, weaving through seaweed and milling around the rocks that speckle the sandy bottom. I pause momentarily. What if the fish tell Madame Cleo we're here?

Nah. Who knows if they can even talk like she can. Mermaids are entirely different from fish, aren't they? And no one else seems worried. Ollie and Jax have already slipped into their cubbies, Maxine is squeezing herself into the giant-sized one with Kayla's help, and Jocelyn is choosing between two centered in the middle. She waves me over.

"Gilly, take this one!" she whispers. "It's free."

"Okay," I whisper back and slip inside just as I hear talking again.

Fairy be, what is that smell? Bologna? A liverwurst sandwich? I look at the hook to my left. Eww…gross! It's someone's gym socks! No wonder Jocelyn gave me this locker! When I get a hold of her…

Wilson, my mouse, slips out of my uniform pocket and begins to squeak in annoyance. I'm sure he can pick up the scent too. "I can't do anything about it," I tell him. "Hold your nose and let's hear what they're saying." I strain against the wood door to listen while holding my nose, which is not very comfortable.

"Well, what would you have us do, *Princess*? Sit back and do nothing?"

Harlow. I can tell by the tone of her voice. Plus, she's being condescending, which is so her…and Jocelyn.

"I didn't say that, Harlow," Princess Ella says diplomatically.

"We appreciate all that you and my stepmother are doing to keep the students safe."

"Safe *and* prepared!" Harlow cuts in.

"Aye! We're using all of the best safety measures," adds Blackbeard. "Me ship has a new crow's nest where a pirate is on guard twenty-four hours a day to watch for any funny business."

"All the doors and windows have been magically enforced, and we've added charms around the school, not unlike the ones Rumpelstiltskin once used to keep everyone out," Flora says. "But ours are stronger, thanks to Harlow."

"I am constantly in my lab whipping up new potions that can be used for both disarming Alva and for keeping his squad at bay should they ever penetrate our walls, but the children must be prepared," Harlow continues. "Tell them, Rapunzel!"

"I agree!" Rapunzel says, to my surprise. "Alva is not to be messed with. You don't know her the way I do. She's tricky and manipulative in ways Rumpelstiltskin is not. Combined, they pose a deadly threat and Fairy Tale Reform School's students must be prepared. That's why I have the RLWs—"

"Raz," Ella cuts in, "that's all well and good, but you have to understand the parents' perspective. They're worried for their children! They want them to come home. This week alone we've received thirty-two letters from parents of students at Royal Academy pleading with Headmistress Olivina and the royal court to allow them pardon during this time."

Harlow snorts. "Royals are such wimps."

I start to laugh, but stop myself. I know it's wrong…but it is funny.

"We have had no such letters sent to Fairy Tale Reform School, I assure you," Harlow tells her.

"Well, that's not entirely true," Professor Wolfington says. "I've had a handful. Just yesterday Gillian Cobbler's mother wrote her, imploring her to come home as well."

How does he know that?

"But she's not going," Flora reminds him. "She hasn't asked us, and I doubt she would. She's the picture of calm during drills, and she's growing into a fine leader."

"A leader with a cloudy relationship with her sister, the poor dear," Madame Cleo interjects. "I see stormy seas ahead for that family."

"So why did you call today's meeting?" Rapunzel asks. "I have classes to teach that my hologram can't possibly handle."

"Of course, we should get going," Snow begins. "We got

some intelligence from someone Rose used to, well, associate with."

The room is quiet.

"I'm not in allegiance with them anymore, as you know," Rose says, her voice tight, "but I thought reaching out could be helpful to the kingdom during this time. And I learned…"

Suddenly, I feel as if I'm moving, as if the entire cube is drifting out to sea, but that's impossible. And yet, I think the row of cubbies is actually being lifted into the air and flown elsewhere. My whole body shifts to the left, and I catch Wilson before he gets thrown across the cubby. I hear a small shriek and know it's Kayla in the cubby next to me. There's no way to see what's going on outside the cubby, but whatever is happening, is happening to all of us. I start to sweat. I want to open this cubby door so badly, but then I'll give myself away and—*AAAH!*

The front door of the cubby begins to open, and I grab hold of a hook to hang on, catching Wilson and myself before we fall several feet. I look out and see that the cubbies have been lifted into the air, have turned sideways, and are now hovering over my teachers' meeting. I've been caught.

My professors and the royal court are staring up at me, and they don't look pleased.

Maxine slides from her cubby and drops to the ground, landing with a thud so hard, it dents the floor, but she seems to be okay. Kayla slides out of her cubby next, but with wings she's able to flutter to the ground. Ollie grabs a hold of one of her legs and let's go as well. Jocelyn, Jax, and I continue to hang on.

"You can come down now," Harlow says tartly. "We can see you."

"No, thanks," Jocelyn says. "We're fine where we are."

Despite our best attempts to hold on, Harlow points her wand at us, and our grips loosen. We are pulled from the cubbies and suspended upside-down in midair. I can move my lips, but the rest of my limbs are frozen.

"Hello, your highnesses," Jax says. "It's a pleasure to see you, as always."

"Jax!" Rapunzel tsks. "How could you? You're a royal. You're supposed to be setting an example." Rapunzel looks at the teachers and the rest of the royal court. "This threat is not a joke. When you're all ready to discuss things seriously, let me know. In the meantime, I have work to do."

"Raz! Wait!" Ella calls to her, but she is already out the door.

Rose shakes her head. "If only the children hadn't interrupted."

I hate her tone. Plus, I'm still bent out of shape at how she once tricked me. "These *kids* have done a lot of good for this kingdom," I point out. I attempt to blow my hair off my face, but it doesn't work. "We have a right to know what you're planning."

"You don't have a right to know anything!" Harlow rages, and Ollie, Kayla, and Maxine are suddenly lifted off the ground and suspended in midair like the rest of us.

"Thanks, Gilly." Ollie's pirate bandanna falls from his head and lands in Madame Cleo's tank.

"You're all meddling again! You're impulsive!" Harlow adds. "Overly confident! You don't think before you act!"

"They're not the only ones," I hear Snow White mutter, but thankfully the former Evil Queen doesn't hear her.

"Why, I have a mind to… I should just…" Harlow's hands start to glow red and a fireball begins to form. Snow White and the royal court rush out of the way. I hear Jocelyn sigh and mumble, "Show-off."

"*Harlow*," Professor Wolfington says soothingly. "Why

don't we all take a deep breath and calm down? Princesses? Maybe you'd like to take a break before we continue?" Blackbeard ushers them over to a formal table where tea service is waiting. "Harlow? Why don't you go to your chambers and conjure a lovely poison spell to settle your nerves?"

"Yes." Harlow scratches her chin. "That does sound soothing. If you'll all excuse me."

"Wait! Sister! Aren't you going to get us down first?" Jocelyn cries.

"Nope." Harlow whips her purple cape around. "You'll fall eventually. You're over Madame Cleo's tank, so you'll be fine." She slams the door behind her.

"Aye! As long as they don't get zapped by an electric eel," Blackbeard points out. "Nasty beasts."

"Blackbeard, is that any way to talk about one of my fellow sea creatures?" Madame Cleo snaps.

Everyone in the room starts bickering. I've never heard them like this before. I blow my purple stripe of hair from my eyes and try to get Maxine's attention, but she's too busy looking at the teachers. Even upside-down, I can tell she's frowning.

Headmistress Flora walks underneath us. "I'm very

disappointed in all of you," she says. "This was a private meeting not meant for children's ears and with our royal court, no less. You need to stop meddling! Didn't what happened in Cloud City teach you anything?" We're all quiet. Headmistress Flora hasn't been this angry in…I don't know how long.

Madame Cleo swims into view. Her mermaid fin is a fiery red. "Detention for all of you!" she says, sounding grumpier than usual. "After Harlow feels like letting you down."

Whoosh!

I free-fall and splash into Madame Cleo's tank, getting tangled in the bamboo reeds. As all of us swim toward the surface, I can't help being disappointed. Once again, we find ourselves treading water.

By official decree of the Royal Court

WANTED

Rumpelstiltskin

Citizens of Enchantasia should be on the lookout for the former headmaster of Fairy Tale Reform School (a.k.a. Enchantasia's resident trickster), who is wanted for conspiring to take over our fair kingdom and breaking Alva, the wicked fairy, out of her stone bonds. If you encounter this individual, or see him with Alva or his Stiltskin Squad, you should contact the Dwarf Police Squad immediately! Do not engage or attempt to take them into custody yourself. They are armed and considered dangerous!

The Dwarf Police Squad would like to remind you: Don't be a troll! If you see something, say something!

CHAPTER 3

You've Been Schooled!

ᖁᖁ

Y ou're late!" Professor Sebastian growls when he sees us.

Jack and Allison Grace, Beauty and the Beast's daughter, are the only two sitting in the room—we have a very small Magical Metamorphosis class. AG's jaw drops when she notices our squishy shoes and very wet clothes. Jack bursts out laughing.

"Where were you?" the professor asks, saying nothing about our awkward appearance.

"We decided to go for a swim, sir," Ollie jokes as Maxine, Jocelyn, Jax, Kayla, and I quickly take our seats. The professor doesn't laugh.

"Um, we were in detention," Kayla tells him.

"Impossible!" the professor barks, but then he thankfully takes a few deep breaths.

We don't need him getting all beastly in the middle of class. AG is pretty good at calming him down, but Beauty is better, and I haven't seen her in the castle today. Come to think of it, it's a little strange that neither one of them was in the meeting in the detention room.

He runs a hand through his long, thick brown hair and raises one very hairy eyebrow at Ollie. "What I mean is, there is no detention in the middle of the day."

"There is if you're caught spying on your teachers while they have a secret meeting with the royal court." Maxine shifts around in her extra-large chair with a giant squeak.

"Maxine!" we scold.

"Sorry!" She blushes. "I can't help but be honest, and I don't like getting in trouble." She looks at the professor again. "We were spying, sir. And we were caught."

I jump in before Maxine can do any more damage. "Actually, sir, I noticed you weren't in the meeting with the rest of the royal court. Can I ask why?"

He slams a stack of scrolls down on his desk. "Some of us believe that focusing on our students' rehabilitation is just as important as chasing after Rumpelstiltskin. If any of you spent half as much time on your grades as you did on battle plans, your scores wouldn't be this terrible!"

Fiddlesticks. I think those are our "Issues of the Fairy World" papers. The paper on top of the stack has a giant red F. That's not good. I didn't put a lot of time into this paper because I was helping Jax draw up a new evacuation plan from the school, but I'm sure I didn't do *that bad*. I wonder whose grade that is?

"You all got F's!" Professor Sebastian thunders, getting wound up again.

Yowza.

Maxine's lower lip trembles. "Are we getting kicked out of the class?"

He whirls around. His chest is heaving up and down. "No. Because then we'd have no class!" He motions to AG and Jack. "Two students is not enough for a Magical Metamorphosis study program, but maybe we shouldn't have one. None of you are doing a very good job undergoing a metamorphosis anyway." He lifts one of the scrolls and begins reading our papers. "Listen to these questions and answers." He clears his throat. "'If you wanted to go the Festival of the

Fairies but didn't have a ride, what would you do?'" He looks at us. "The majority of you answered, 'I'd steal a ride or hide in someone's carriage to get there.' That's not what you do!"

I don't dare ask why. Is hiding in the back of a perfectly good empty carriage so wrong?

"And this one," Professor Sebastian continues. "'If you were in the middle of the village and saw a troll break into the Three Little Pigs restaurant, what would you do?'" He looks up. "Ollie answered: 'Follow him into the store, tie him up with magical binds, and question him about what he's doing there.'"

The rest of us mumble in agreement.

"No!" Professor Sebastian sounds exasperated. "The correct answer is: 'Call the Dwarf Police Squad for help.'"

"But what if we're able to help on our own?" Jax asks.

"That's not your job! Your job is... Well, I don't know what any of your jobs are yet, because you're all too busy worrying about what's going on with Alva and Rumpelstiltskin to figure that out!"

"Sounds like someone else I know," AG mutters as she stares at the top of her desk and fiddles with a quill. I hear our teacher growl, but AG doesn't back down. "It's true! You spent years tailing the little twerp, locked away in your office reading books and trying locator spells. After what he pulled in Cloud City, can you blame any of us for trying to prepare for the day he shows up here?"

I brace for impact. And by impact, I mean a roar of explosion from Professor Sebastian.

Instead, he's quiet. So quiet, I can hear the ticking of the cuckoo clock on the wall behind his gold desk and the hum of Miri's mirror behind his head. (I feel like she's always watching and listening even when her mirror is dark.) He strokes his beard, takes a seat on his desk, and looks at us.

AG crouches down in her chair, and Jax and I glance at each other nervously. What is he going to do?

"You're right," he says, and I nearly fall out of my chair. "I wasted too many years worrying about that man and thought too little of myself." He stares out a stained glass window that has a view of the empty courtyard. "While your mother studied books and taught you about the world, I locked myself away to hunt a man who had already imprisoned me for far too long." He looks at me in particular. "It's easy to be consumed by anger. It's harder to learn to let things go. I guess I don't want the same for any of you."

Who is this imposter, and what has he done with my

teacher? Should I poke him to make sure he's not Hologram Professor Sebastian? Because this doesn't sound like the cranky pants we all know...and er, tolerate.

"I'm sorry, AG. You're right about me," he tells his daughter.

"I am?" AG asks.

"I want you all to use your time at Fairy Tale Reform School wisely. Who do you want to be when you leave this place? This is why I give you tests like the one you just had. Not to torture you, but to prepare you. We can all worry about when that man may try to break down the door, or you can think about what you will do with your future. In the end, we all know that evil never really wins. So what will you do when the dust settles? Who are you?"

If I wasn't so wet and waterlogged, I might hug the man. He brings up a good point... *Oh no, Maxine, don't!*

"Thank you, sir!" She tackles him in a big bear hug. "I needed that today! Everyone has been so cranky and down. We should just be happy when we have the chance."

AG stifles a giggle, but Professor Sebastian is straight-faced as he pries Maxine off him. He smooths out his red, velvet jacket. "Very true, Maxine. So what do you plan to do when you leave FTRS?"

Maxine gives him a toothy grin. "I'm thinking I'd like to open up a school for toddlers, like Mother Goose did. I have a way with children once they get used to my appearance, and I think I'd be quite good at playing games like Duck, Duck, Goose, and singing nursery rhymes."

He strokes his beard. "I could see that."

"So could I," I say, and Peaches quacks in agreement. I didn't even realize Maxine had her hidden in a bag by her desk. The prince doesn't say anything about it though. Instead, he looks at me.

"And what about you, Gillian? Where do you see yourself?"

I think for a moment before speaking. "I think I'd make a good police chief. We all know Pete drops the ball a lot. He's never around when we *really* need him. I'm good in a fight, and I know how to navigate a battle…most times." I try hard not to think about what happened in Cloud City with Anna. "I think I'd be good for Enchantasia."

Jax grins. "Chief Cobbler. It has a nice ring to it."

Maxine wipes her nose. "You'd make a good chief! I'd vote for you!"

"I'm not sure I see it—feels so rigid and dull," Jocelyn says. "I'd rather open a dark magic shop and teach people how to defend themselves like Red Riding Hood, but to each her own."

I'm feeling pretty confident till I hear Jack snicker. I turn around.

"No offense, but no one is going to name you police chief," he says.

"That's rude of you to say," Jax starts.

"She's a thief!" Jack reminds us. "They'd never put a criminal in charge of public safety. The royal court would never go for it, and you all know it."

AG frowns, her porcelain-white face crumpling. "Jack might be right."

"This kingdom would be lucky to have me," I argue. "I've faced many villains, and I'm still here. The people would love me."

"While that might be true, Mr. Spriggins has a point," Professor Sebastian says. "This kingdom might have a hard time feeling comfortable with a former thief in a position of power."

"Forget I even brought it up." I fold my arms, focusing my attention on the window so I don't have to make eye contact with anyone. "It was a stupid idea anyway."

"No, it's not!" Maxine says. "It's a wonderful idea! You

shouldn't give it up because Jack or even Professor Sebastian doesn't think it can happen. You have to *make* it happen!"

Jocelyn rolls her eyes. "I think I found a better career for Maxine—inspirational speaker."

We all laugh, even me, and then I feel bad. Maxine hangs her head. "I'm just kidding, Maxine," I say. "But life isn't all sunshine and fairy gardens."

"But it could be." Maxine is not deterred. She leans forward, making her desk wobble. "If we all focused on what we have right now, instead of worrying about all that could go wrong, we'd be so much happier."

"Here she goes again," Ollie mumbles.

"Professor Sebastian is giving us a chance to think about our futures." Maxine continues, "We should be exploring our passions and walking through the village, thinking about where we see ourselves. We should be trying new jobs on for size! Not worrying about battles!"

"Maxine is right," Professor Sebastian says, and my head almost spins off. "You all need a dose of reality. Being cooped up in this castle with all these Wanted scrolls and battle drills is making you forget there is still a life out there that people are living!"

"Yes!" Maxine agrees.

"So to make up for how terribly you all did on your test, you're going to live the real-world version of it for bonus points to bring up your grades." Professor Sebastian gives us a beastly grin. "Your assignment: an outing in the village to explore potential career paths. I'll clear it with Professor Flora," he adds, stroking his beard some more, "but I think Maxine has had a wonderful idea. You will interview people in your potential lines of work, and then I'll give you some money to buy breakfast and lunch. We will see how you do interacting with the public and working with a budget. It will be a great exercise!"

Maxine beams.

Kayla is taking notes. "How long should the essay on our experience be, sir?"

I glare at her. Who said anything about an essay?

"No essay! You'll give an oral presentation on the experience. This way I can ask follow-up questions." Everyone begins talking at once. "Now, I must end class early. I have a lunch date with Beauty, but I will be in touch about your field trip date. I'm sure I can schedule it this week."

"Nice going, Maxine," Jocelyn whispers as we gather our things.

"It *is* nice, isn't it?" Maxine asks dreamily.

"Gillian?" Professor Sebastian calls as everyone files out. "Hold on, will you? I'd like to give you a second assignment."

I get two things for homework when they all have one? What gives! "Sir?"

"I'm going to have Miri speak with Pete at the Dwarf Police headquarters," says Professor Sebastian, staring down at me. "Maybe if you interview him and learn more about being a police chief, it will help you decide if this is a job you want to someday fight for." He puts a hand on my shoulder. "Important things should always be fought for."

I'm surprised, but I try not to show it. "Thank you, sir."

"You're welcome," he says and actually smiles. His teeth are really white. "Oh, and Gillian? Let's get a date on the calendar for you and me to talk more about Rumpelstiltskin. If you and I put our heads together, I think we can learn how to separate the man from the myth and figure out his weaknesses." He raises an eyebrow. "That could be the real clue to beating him at his own game, you know."

I smile. "I'd like that."

Beast or man, Professor Sebastian is much wiser than I realized.

CHAPTER 4

Pink Power!

It's been way too long since we've had an RLW meeting," Maxine says as we walk into the only rose-scented room in the castle. The air is thick with the mist that comes from hairspray, and everywhere we look is pink. It is, after all, a Royal Lady-in-Waiting's signature color.

As if being in a royal fan club wasn't bad enough.

"Too long? We had two meetings last"—*Cough! Cough!* I wave the hairspray mist away from my face—"week!"

"Yes." Maxine slides her pink RLW sash, which is filling up with club badges (*Pruning 101, Napkin-Folding Skills, The Art of Using a Handkerchief*) over her large head. "That feels like forever ago. This meeting is the only still-normal thing at FTRS." I roll my eyes without meaning to, and Maxine waves a grayish finger at me. "You know it's true! This is the only place where it's okay to be happy and plan parties and care about table arrangements. The rest of the school is obsessed with a possible war."

Whoosh! If I'm not mistaken a thorny flower stem just flew between Maxine and me at the speed of light. *Whoosh! Whoosh! Whoosh!* Three more flower stems come straight for us, and I pull Maxine to the floor. I look up to see the stems have hit the stone wall above our heads and cracked it. What in the name of fairy is going on?

"Brilliant, Raza! Well done!" Tessa, our RLW leader, steps out of the shadows clapping her hands. I sit up in surprise. "The stem completely went into the wall this time. I think our modifications to the flower darts worked well." She steps over us and pulls the stems from the stone. "And look! They can still be used again."

Raza daintily holds up the bottom of her skirt as she runs over. She peers at the dart closely with her beady goblin eyes. "Wonderful! This brings my batch to forty-two. Enough for each RLW to have two." Several RLWs gather round to see. Maxine and I join them.

Tessa frowns. "I don't think two is enough. We should all

get to work making more darts." She claps her hands. "Chop, chop, ladies! We don't have all day. To your stations!" The girls rush to our RLW tables. My eyes widen in surprise.

Usually the tables are set with the finest china and linens we have at FTRS. The tablescape is always pink, and the theme depends on each week's RLW lesson, but today the table is bare except for a black tablecloth. I quickly read the hand-written scroll adorned with flowers and ribbons that sits on the table.

Today's lesson is…weapon making?

This club just got interesting.

I walk over to join my club mates.

"Wait!" Maxine cries, pulling at her sash in frustration. "Today's lesson is supposed to be 'How to Plan the Perfect Fairy Garden Party.' Not weapon making!"

"Under the circumstances, we changed today's theme," says Tessa as she fiddles with the pearls around her neck. Raza stands next to her in a show of solidarity. I notice her pointy goblin ears have several pairs of earrings in them. Instead of her traditional jewels and pearls, they are tiny silver…swords? "There is no time for party planning when the castle is under attack!"

Maxine groans loudly before sitting on a pink, tufted

ottoman. "Nooooo, not you guys too! This was the one safe space I had!" She drops her head into her hands.

"What is she whining about?" Raza asks me.

I open my mouth to speak, but Maxine cuts me off. "Whining? I'm not whining! I'm ready to plan a party! We have one for Kayla's family in one week, if you've forgotten, and we've done nothing to prepare for it. How are guests going to know how to shrink down to fairy size if we don't decorate a basket with small, scented scrolls that explain it? How will we decorate the fairy garden if we don't start making paper lanterns and gathering fireflies to light it?"

My roommate's voice gets shriller with every point she makes. We begin to back up as she looks like she might charge.

"She's losing it," Ollie whispers to me. His Royal Lad-in-Waiting sash is glowing red and has skulls and crossbones painted on it. "Someone better go get Peaches to calm her down."

"There's no time." I'm afraid to move.

"Hey!" AG runs in and takes a spot next to me. "What did I miss?" Her eyes focus in on the flower stems on the ground and on the table. "Are those...weapons? I thought RLWs didn't do that sort of thing."

"Apparently, we do now," I tell her.

"Cool," AG says in awe.

But Maxine does not find it cool. "How are we going to know what to order from the kitchens if we don't put together a menu?" she shouts. "Do we serve mini cinnamon rolls or Bundt cakes with strawberry cream? What tea should we serve? How do we decide, if we're too busy making flower darts? We need a menu!" She slams her hand down on the table, and the darts shoot straight into the air before they rain down on the room. Girls shriek and scatter.

"Maxine? What is going on?" Rapunzel runs into the room wearing a lilac pantsuit. "Are you all right?"

There are a few gasps as everyone notices our club advisor is wearing *pants*. Rapunzel's bodice is purple leather, and her pants are slim and covered by boots that climb above her knees.

"What's the matter?" Rapunzel asks, and Maxine bursts into tears. Rapunzel looks at the rest of us for answers. We all shrug.

I speak up. "She wants to plan a party."

"I want to plan the *fairy garden* party," Maxine corrects me. "Is that so wrong? That's what RLWs do—plan parties! Make things pretty! Make the royal court feel special when they visit! We don't make weapons!" She sobs louder, and Rapunzel hands her a handkerchief. Maxine blows into it loudly.

"Don't cry," Rapunzel says. "We *are* going to plan a party."

"We are?" we all ask.

"Yes!" Rapunzel says. "It's our job. We are grateful to Angelina, Kayla, and her sisters for all they've done, especially in terms of tracking Rumpelstiltskin. It would be disrespectful not to honor them with this party. We will just have to keep things simple. We have other more important tasks at hand as well."

Maxine wipes her eyes with the back of her hand. "What's more important than their party?"

"Building an arsenal of weapons to defend our school and our royal court, of course!" Rapunzel takes a seat on her club advisor throne and smooths her pants. "An RLW's job is to serve. In times of war, we have different ways of serving."

"No." Maxine shakes her head. "Not you too."

"I'm so pleased with the darts Tessa and Raza created," Rapunzel says with pride. "They are the perfect weapon. If we place them in flower pots around the school and on the grounds, we will always have a weapon at the ready should the need arise. We need to make sure we have as many as we can by the time of the party." Her face darkens. "Times of celebration tend to be the perfect moment to invade the fairy tale community. Villains love to make an entrance or come in undetected when royals' guards are down. But no more!" She raises her fist into the air, and the RLWs thunder with applause. "A new dawn of RLWs is coming! We are warriors who will protect our court and our school at all costs. We will continue to learn to fight and build weapons. That is our true mission now. Parties are an afterthought, I'm afraid."

"But…" Maxine begins.

Rapunzel looks at her. "I'm happy to let you be in charge of the fairy party since it seems to mean so much to you. I'd much rather have Tessa and Raza on weapon duty."

"Raza and I came up with an idea for a rock infused with magical powers that can be called from any location," Tessa says with glee. "You whistle and it comes flying toward you and can be redirected to hit an enemy."

"Oooh…" the other girls say.

AG raises her hand. "I'll help Maxine plan the party. I'd like to make sure the day is lovely for Kayla's family."

"Thank you, AG," Rapunzel says. "I'm sure you two can get it done in time."

"Usually it takes the whole club *weeks* to plan such an event, but two people can do it in one week, I guess, if they have to." Maxine gives Ollie and me a look.

Oh, fiddlesticks. I'd much rather make rock weapons! But Maxine is my roommate. "Fine, I'll help."

"Me too." Ollie sounds as disappointed as I do.

"Wonderful," Raz says, but she's already looking at the darts. "Have fun planning." She claps her hands. "Ladies? The rest of us should do a quick martial arts warm-up before we return to weapons making. I want to make sure all of you know how to do a proper roundhouse kick. Let me demonstrate." Rapunzel steps back and lets her right leg fly through the air with a swift side kick. "If I had known how to do one of these earlier in life, maybe I could have thwarted Alva myself." Everyone nods in agreement. "Okay, let's try it together."

Girls run around the room in search of open space to practice. Maxine, AG, Ollie, and I aren't sure what to do.

"Oh, you four can go," Rapunzel says. "I'm sure you'd rather work on party plans somewhere quiet." She kicks the air again and focuses on the girls. "On my count, RLWs. One…two…and three!"

The four of us walk out to avoid all the flailing limbs. Maxine storms ahead of us. "I take it back," she grumbles. "RLW meetings are no fun at all."

CHAPTER 5

Field Trip

N ow remember, we are all meeting at the Humpty Dumpty clock tower at precisely three in the afternoon," Beauty instructs us as the Pegasus carriage begins its final descent. As our official chaperone, Beauty is the one in charge. Professor Sebastian told us he "doesn't do field trips." I guess she'll be reporting back to him about our behavior.

Through the opening at the back of the carriage, I see us break through the clouds and the tops of tiny boots, teacups, and cottages come into view.

"You have three hours to conduct your interviews and experience village life." Beauty gives us all a pointed look. "I don't want to hear of any horseplay or hanging out at the sweet shop. Your professor gave you each specific instructions on what he'd like you to do while you're here. Does everyone have their scrolls?"

We hold them up.

"I'll be helping out at Mother Goose's Nursery School," Maxine says, flashing us all a toothy grin.

"I'm meeting with the head of the royal navy," Ollie says, his chest puffing with pride. "I wonder if there's time for a quick voyage." He stares off into the distance. "Oh, how I'd like to take the wheel of one of their ships." He looks at us. "I'd bring it back, of course."

Jocelyn reads from her scroll. "It says he wants me to check out the healers' shop." She rolls her eyes. "He thinks maybe I have a future in concocting healing potions. Sounds dull."

"So does mine," Allison Grace says with a deep sigh. "I'm having tea with a group of royals in the village. How is that a career choice?"

Beauty frowns. "I agree, that's not very helpful. Why don't you check out one of the schools in town and see if you can observe there instead? I've always thought you'd make a great teacher."

"Okay!" AG looks relieved. "But *you're* telling Father about the switch." Beauty winks at her.

"I'm headed to the market to talk to the farmers about their crops," Jack says. "Professor knows my dream is to own a farm."

"And I'm meeting with village business owners to discuss any concerns they have with the royal court," Jax tells us. "As a future leader, I need to practice meeting with my people and listening to their needs."

"I'm visiting a commune of fairies that I've never met before to discuss fairy/human relations, which is something I'm quite interested in," Kayla says. "I can't wait to tell them about Mother's return!"

Everyone looks at me.

"And I have an appointment with Pete at the Dwarf Police Squad headquarters." Jack snickers, and I glare at him. "Maybe I should take you with me, so he can lock you up. There is no way you're going to make it three hours in the village without stealing something."

Jack narrows his eyes at me. "Want to make a bet?"

Beauty steps between us as the carriage lands with a soft thud near the village's Pegasus stables. "No one is stealing anything." She begins passing out slips of parchment. "You all have lunch vouchers that can be used at any number of establishments in the village. They're good for something to eat and drink. They cannot be used to buy trinkets of any kind. If you purchase anything today, you will be expected to show me proof of purchase."

I look at my voucher. I can eat at Three Little Pigs, the Pied Piper Luncheonette, Under the Sea Seafood, or Muffin Man Meats.

Ollie groans. "I don't think any of these places have patty-cakes. They're my favorite."

The back of the carriage is unlocked, and workers place wooden stairs so we can step out. I look around. There are already two queues of people waiting for Pegasus rides to various places like the royal court or a day excursion to a place called Nottingham. People are walking by the stables on their way to appointments or to go shopping. A fleet of magic carpets with a student driver flies unsteadily by while a group of school children singing "Miss Mary Mack" skip past us.

"Have fun! And watch the time!" says Beauty, gathering a basket and some books and heading off.

"Should we meet up for lunch after our appointments?" Jax asks. "Mine shouldn't take more than an hour. Should give us time to get food and look around."

"Whatever." Jocelyn flicks lint off her black cape. It still kills me that she's the only student at FTRS who doesn't have to wear these blue uniforms! All she has to wear is our school crest on her black gown. "It's not like we have money to buy anything fun. Harlow said, 'It's not appropriate for me to give you money to spend when no one else has any.' It's like she's gone all soft or something."

"I have a bit of money with me," Maxine says sheepishly, and we all look at her. "Mother sent me birthday money months ago, and I never spent it."

"How?" Ollie looks aghast. "I would have spent all my money on patty-cakes if I had any." He sniffs the air. "I think there's a cart nearby making a fresh batch."

Jax grabs Ollie's arm. "No patty-cakes for you. Not after what happened last time."

Ollie blushes. He almost got us caught one time with his patty-cakes obsession. In the distance, we hear the clock tower toll. "Guess we should get to our appointments," he says.

"Then we'll all meet back here for lunch and to take Maxine shopping," AG says pleasantly.

I head into the heart of the village, passing some of my favorite shops, like Gnome-olia Bakery and Red's

Ready-for-Anything Shoppe, and I do my best not to look east, where I know the streets will lead me home to 2 Boot Way. As much as I'd love to see my brothers and sisters, if Mother knew I was in town, she'd cook my favorite meal (chicken potpie) and give me a thousand reasons why I should stay home and not go back to school.

A crowd of people up ahead are watching a *Happily Ever After Scrolls* employee nail a scroll to a post near the town square. There is a lot of murmuring and worried glances, and I notice one child crying. I move in closer to read what was posted, and my stomach drops.

Happily Ever After Scrolls
Brought to you by FairyWeb—
Enchantasia's Number One News Source!

Is Enchantasia Still a Safe Place to Live? Why I Fear for Our Safety

Editorial by Princess Rose

Fairy be! Princess Rose is going to get people wound up like a top! I wonder what the rest of the royal court thinks about her writing editorials for *Happily Ever After Scrolls*?

The clock strikes in the square again, and I know I only have a few minutes before I'm supposed to meet Pete. I hurry past the people reading Princess Rose's editorial and go straight to the Dwarf Police Squad headquarters. I've actually never been inside. Pete always apprehended me at home or on location, but today, I'm walking inside as a free citizen and, er…

ELF Construction is doing repairs to the front of the police headquarters. The shiny gold sign is tarnished and bent, and one of the doors to the building is busted in along with a window. The bricks on the front are crumbling in places, and it's not from decay.

"Yep, you caused that, Cobbler, with you and your pal Jax's rogue magic carpet ride," Pete drawls, walking out a smaller door on the side to greet me. "How do you like your handiwork?"

I stare down at him. He's tinier when he's not on his horse. Olaf, his sidekick, isn't with him. Pete's goatee has been trimmed so it no longer reaches his chest and covers his badge, which he wears like it's his name tag—CHIEF OF THE DWARF

POLICE SQUAD, PETER STUBRIDGE. Stubridge? That's his last name? I never knew that. Several ribbons are hanging from his gold badge, and I notice they're honors from the royal court: "For exemplary bravery in a time of chaos," reads a red one. "For putting the needs of the royal court first," announces a yellow ribbon. "First prize in the annual police squad chili cook-off," says the blue one.

"What are you looking at?" Pete growls. "Come in, already." He walks ahead of me down a long hallway. "But don't case the joint. I'm still not sure why Professor Sebastian thinks it's a good idea for us to talk."

I follow Pete into what must be the command center. There are maps peppered with tiny pins and Wanted scrolls of every villain in the kingdom wallpapering the room, including one for some outlaw named Robin Hood. I whip around at the sound of Miri's voice, and sure enough, one of her framed mirrors is glowing purple in the squad room.

"The royal court feels that is an unnecessary lead to follow at this time," she tells a small elf with a long, red beard. "But thank you for checking in with us!"

The mirror goes dark, but I'm left to wonder: Who do they have a lead on? Rumpelstiltskin?

"Keep up!" Pete grumbles. "I don't have all day to talk to kids about school projects."

Next, we walk past a room full of cells—it's the jail! It's packed with ogres, elves, sprites, and even a few fairies. An elf catches me staring and throws his lunch plate at me. I duck, forgetting the plate will just bounce off the bars.

Pete chuckles. "Yeah, I wouldn't get too close." He gives the prisoners the evil eye. "They get kind of grumpy when they're locked up for almost a week. But none of you are getting out till you tell me what happened to Troll Bridge Toll Plaza!" Pete looks at me, his black eyes gleaming in wonder. "The whole stone building is missing, like it magically vanished!" We hear snickering, and he turns around and rattles the bars. "You won't think it's so funny when I leave you in here another week. That mush you're getting fed will taste really good after you've had it for fourteen days!" They throw a few more plates at the bars, and Pete motions to me to move. "Let's go talk in my office. Give them some time to think about their actions."

When we reach Pete's office, I see his name on the door above his head, but the doorknob is low enough for him to reach it. He opens the door and lets me in first.

"Take a seat," he says, walking around to the back and jumping on a chair. He pumps the chair till he's seated high above me. I take a seat on the opposite chair and look around. There are portraits of him with Snow White everywhere—they do go way back—and ones of him and the royal court at what looks like a knighting ceremony. Someone has drawn a childlike portrait of Pete that he has framed on his desk. It's really sweet. Maybe I misjudged him.

"So why are you bothering me with a school project?" Pete leans back in his chair and folds his arms over his chest. "You don't even like me."

That's true. "That's not true," I say diplomatically. "I've always admired how, you've, er, managed to stay one step ahead of me when it came to my pickpocketing." Also not true. I always prided myself on outrunning him when I could.

Pete eyes me suspiciously. "You always gave me a hard time."

He's got my number. "I know, and I'm sorry for that, but if it weren't for you, I'd still be on the streets, rather than a semireformed thief who's making positive changes." That part is true. Pete still doesn't look convinced though. "That's why Professor Sebastian suggested I meet with you today. So I could learn more about your career."

He looks as if he just smelled a rotten turnip. "Why would you want to do that?"

I stare at the plaques and portraits of Pete that represent his accomplishments. I hear the criminals groaning in the other room and think of the commotion going on in the command center. The thrill of tracking down a villain. The idea of catching a bad guy before they can get away with something. Stopping someone like Rumpelstiltskin. "Because I want to be you."

For a moment, there's a strange silence as Pete and I look at each other. Then Pete bursts out laughing. "*You* want to be *me*? You're pulling my leg!" He spins around in his chair. "Where is Olaf? He has to hear this!" He's laughing so hard, I fear he's going to fall off his chair.

"It's not a joke," I say, getting annoyed. "I want your job someday."

He stops laughing, and his face grows serious. "That will never happen."

"Why not?" I demand.

His eyes widen. "Because you're a thief! Or at least, you were one! A good one, at that, who wound up at Fairy Tale Reform School. Former thieves do not become the head of the Dwarf Police Squad. And besides, you're not a dwarf."

"There are a lot of people in this building who are not dwarves," I remind him. "Maybe you and Snow started this organization, but now anyone can be part of it, and I think I'd be a great police chief." He snorts. "Think about it: I know how a thief thinks because I was one. Who better to do the job than me? And besides, I've already caught several villains you couldn't."

He glares at me. "And you also let some important ones get away, like Rumpelstiltskin. Twice." He leans forward. "How do we know you aren't working with him right now?"

"Because I'm not evil," I say coldly. How dare Pete put me in the same category as Stiltskin? "I'm on our side."

"Your kid sister ain't." Pete picks up a pencil and starts to chew on it. "Your sister is as sinister as he is. So I hear."

He's trying to get under my skin, but I'm not going to let him. "She's made her choice, and I've made mine." My voice is like steel. "I know I could do your job. Yelling at prisoners and eating patty-cakes all day doesn't look that hard."

He sighs. "You think this job is a piece of cake, don't you? You have no idea what I do day in and day out in this place."

I stifle a yawn. Pete's never been what I'd call a go-getter.

If he thinks he can convince me he works hard, he's got another think coming.

His face grows serious. "The job isn't just about battling villains. The biggest responsibility is listening to every person that comes to you with a problem, no matter how small or petty it is, and making them feel as if they've been heard."

I snort. "Yeah, and you've done a great job of that with me over the years."

Pete slams down his fist. "You don't want to listen? You might as well just leave."

If that's how he's going to be, I'm out of here. "Fine! I'll let the professor know you were extremely helpful." Pete's right eyebrow begins to twitch. I march to the door. "But if I were you, I wouldn't get too comfortable with this office." I tap the name plate. "One day, this office is going to be mine. I'm sure of it." His face pales as I slam the door behind me.

✦✳✦

Even a hot, steaming stack of pancakes at Three Little Pigs can't cheer me up. Everyone is talking about how amazing their meetings went. Maxine was invited to intern at Mother

Goose's, and AG made some empowered speech at her ladies' tea about the changing face of beauty before observing a class at Jack of All Trades School. Ollie swears the royal navy has asked him to someday captain a ship, and Jax is confident he made some real headway with the village business owners. They let Jocelyn mix some poison recipes, which seems to have made her very happy (I suspect they tossed them as soon as she left), and Jack got to talk to a group of farmers.

"How did yours go, Gilly?" Maxine asks, her eyes wide and hopeful. Everyone looks at me.

"Pete is a dim-witted, micro-mini troll!" I complain, and everyone gasps, including the troll serving us.

"We don't like that type of language in here." He narrows his one eye at me.

"We're terribly sorry," Jax says. "It won't happen again." The troll lumbers away.

"Told you he wouldn't understand." Jack steals a pancake from someone's plate since he's already finished his own. "There's no way anyone in this kingdom will let you become a police chief."

"I don't want to talk about this anymore." I turn away from the group and look at the other diners, all of whom are still giving me the evil eye for my comment. My cheeks flush as guilt sets in. I push my plate away. "I think I'm going to go for a walk."

"We'll go with you," Jocelyn suggests. "We're finished here anyway."

"We are?" Ollie has a mouth full of pancake. When he's not looking, Jack swipes the last forkful from his plate. Ollie glances down. "I guess we are."

We put our food vouchers in the middle of the table, and I add the few coins I have on me for a tip for the waiter.

"Come on," Maxine says. "There's a new shop right down the block that I want to see. It looks cool!" We hurry along behind her, sidestepping horses galloping down the street and villagers on their lunch breaks.

"I wonder what's got her so excited?" Jax asks. I shrug. "Don't worry, thief. Er, former thief. Pete is not the be-all and end-all. If you want that job bad enough, maybe the royal court can make it happen for you."

I semi-smile and stop short behind Maxine. "Thanks."

"*This* is where you wanted to go?" Jocelyn asks. Broken doors, tables, and lamps litter the front of the store. "A junk shop?"

"It's not a junk shop." Maxine points to the rusted sign above the cottage door. "It's Javier's Jewels and Exotic Treasures!" She opens the door. "Let's see what's inside."

"I hope it's not a villain," Ollie whispers as he passes what appears to be a shrunken head hanging from the door. "This place gives me the creeps."

Inside, the cottage has a musty smell. Dust swirls around the piles of broken windows, used potion bottles, and tables of small mirrors, feathers, quills, and other trinkets that don't appear to work. It's so cluttered, you can barely move down the aisles. There's not another soul in the joint, which is making me wary.

AG blows dust off a stack of books. "A thousand and one ways to cast a sleeping curse." She shudders while Jocelyn reaches for the book. "Is this a villain shop?"

"Absolutely not!" comes a high-pitched voice. We jump as a tall, thin man appears out of nowhere. He's wearing a bright suit bejeweled with sparkly beads that are also woven into his long, white beard. This must be Javier. "We carry all kinds of treasures, but never discriminate between hero and villain."

"How do you get the stuff?" asks Ollie, touching what appears to be a wooden mermaid from the front of a ship.

Javier pulls at his chin. "Oh, people give them to me for various reasons. You never know what you'll find. See anything you like?"

I'm just about to say no and rush us out of there when Maxine squeals.

"Look at this!" She holds up a rusty can. "I had one of these when I was a wee ogress."

Jack looks at it closely. "A broken bottle?"

"I think it's a small lampshade," says Ollie.

"It's junk, is what it is," says Jocelyn.

"It's a lamp!" Maxine turns it over in her fingers. It has a thin spout and a small brown lid, but it's so dirty and rusted I can't make out any other details. "My father brought me one just like it from one of his journeys." Her smile fades. "When our home was burned down in the Troll War, it was lost." She holds it to her chest, and some of the rust falls off it. "I have to have this. How much?"

Javier pulls at his beard. "Oh, I'm afraid that's pricey. It's very valuable."

He's lying. "It's rusted and old," I say. "You're just trying to make a buck off a group of kids."

"That's extortion," Jax declares, and we all agree.

"I'm not! It's a rare find!" Javier comes closer and takes it from Maxine's hands. "I didn't even realize it was in the shop. Sure, it's dirty, but a little elbow grease will make it shiny and gold again. I'm not sure I could part with it. Its owner said it's a magic lamp, but no matter how many times I try, I can't seem to make a genie appear."

"You're fibbing," Jocelyn blurts out.

"I'm not." Javier begins walking off with it. "It's not for sale. I'm sorry."

"Please!" Maxine begs. "I will give you all my birthday money. I have to have it."

"You said this so-called genie has never appeared for you," Jax reminds him. "Maybe there isn't one in there, and you're just wasting your time."

"There definitely isn't one," Jack scoffs. "Genies aren't real. Everyone knows that."

Javier looks thoughtful for a moment. "Maybe you're right." He hands Maxine the lamp. "It's yours. For the right price."

"Thank you! Thank you!" Maxine says, emptying her pockets and forking over all her bills and loose change.

I shake my head and exchange glances with Jocelyn. Javier won't regret this, but Maxine definitely will.

INVITATION FOR ALL STUDENTS
AT FAIRY TALE REFORM SCHOOL

You are cordially invited to attend a

FAIRY GARDEN PARTY

Honoring esteemed fairies:

Angelina, Kayla, Emma Rose, and Brooke Lynn

Date: This Saturday

Place: The fairy garden (prepare to shrink!)

Thrown by: The Royal Ladies-in-Waiting

Maxine and Allison Grace

Note from Rapunzel: Due to the current villain climate, students will be allowed to bring their weapons with them to the party, but they will be held at the door. Remember: If you see something, say something!

CHAPTER 6

Fairy Good Party Planning

I wave the invite in front of Maxine's face. "I cannot believe you changed the invitation!"

"Hey! I can't see!" Maxine tries to duck and weave around the scroll so she can continue cleaning her lamp at our dorm room desk. She's got some sort of polish concoction, a few potions, ELF Cleaning Spray, and various rags and brushes laid out in front of her. Peaches is sitting on the desk watching Maxine scrub. And scrub. And scrub. Occasionally, Peaches tries to eat one of the brushes, and then Maxine shoos her away.

Wilson pokes his small, pink nose out of my pocket and sneezes.

Maxine's concoction smells like Ollie's feet. "Maxine, you

need to open a window. That smell might kill us!" I crank open the stained glass window and let some fresh air in.

Maxine throws the rag in disgust. "And it's not even working either! Look at it!" She holds her lamp up to the light. It's still the same brown, but now there are patches of green on there as well. I think she's making things worse. "Plus, I can't get the cap loose." She twists the top, but it doesn't budge. "I just want to see what's inside. It sounds hollow." She shakes it. "But I want to know for sure!"

Miri the Magic Mirror crackles and comes to life, swirling with purple and blue colors. "Hello, Fairy Tale Reform School! A quick note, following the fairy garden party, early evening gym classes will be canceled due to Professor Edom's prediction that we're in for a fierce thunderstorm."

"Ooh!" Maxine looks at me. "It wasn't supposed to rain today. Maybe it's actually the typhiras! Will you come outside with me tonight and look for them in the storm?"

"Maxine, for the last time, they're not real!" I say wearily. "Just like that lamp of yours doesn't hold any magic." Wilson sniffs in agreement.

Maxine sets her jaw and continues rubbing the lamp. "You're wrong about the typhiras. They're real! I wish I could see one and prove it to you! And hey…is the lamp glowing?"

I run over to the table, and we both peer at the lamp. "I don't see any glow," I say, feeling badly. I don't mean to be so down on her dreams…even if they're unrealistic.

"I guess I was imagining it." Maxine sighs. "I know you don't think this lamp is magical, but it's still special. If I could just clean it up, it would look like the one I had when I was little." She puts it down and opens a jar of purple paste. "This is my last shot. I whipped this up in the potion lab. It's got gingerroot, beet juice, and lemon." She smears the paste all over the lamp, then places it in a small sack. "Maybe if I leave it on, it will work its magic." She places the sack in a bag overflowing with bottles of glitter, pink and red scarves, and lots of tape. "I really need to get going if we're going to finish setting up the fairy party."

I wave the invitation again. "Speaking of which, you changed the invite and now it looks like you and AG planned everything."

"We *did*." Maxine places her RLW sash over her head. "Tessa and Raza have been too busy learning kung fu to make a single swan napkin or papier-mâché lantern. The rest of the club is practicing self-defense with Rapunzel around the clock."

"Why didn't you tell me when you were meeting?" I ask, feeling guilty.

"You don't like being an RLW, and I know you're worried about Anna." Maxine shrugs. "I didn't want to bother you."

Now I feel even worse.

"We tried going to Headmistress Flora and Harlow to get some extra help, but they're only concerned with tracking down Rumpelstiltskin, so they didn't care either. AG and I have been up past midnight working by firefly light trying to do it all. So yes, I put our names on all the invites. And now, I have to finish planning a party no one is even looking forward to." She grabs her sack and heads to the door. "Are you even coming?"

"Yes. Professor Sebastian said attendance is mandatory." And I could use some extra points since my oral presentation on my meeting with Pete wasn't exactly met with rave reviews. I basically spent three minutes railing against the police squad and complaining about how none of us were ever going to get jobs because former villains will never be trusted. Needless to say, my sentiment did not go over well. "Why don't I help you finish setting up?"

Maxine smiles gratefully. "Thanks. I want everything to be perfect for Kayla and her family."

"So do I," I agree.

Maxine wasn't kidding about the rest of the RLWs being MIA for the party planning. When we shrink down to fairy size and enter the fairy garden to finish decorating, AG looks so overwhelmed, I think she might get beastly.

"Only half the tablecloths are on the tables, the fireflies haven't arrived yet to light the lanterns, and the chef told me he forgot to make cinnamon rolls," AG tells us. "That means we have nothing sweet to serve, and my mother isn't even sure the royal court is coming because the Dwarf Police Squad said it's a security risk for them to shrink to the size of a water goblet!"

I look around at the beautiful garden with its mini fountains, fairy lights hanging from trees, and beautiful weeping willows. AG and Maxine did a great job. This party could be the most stunning FTRS has ever seen, and no one will be here to see it. "Pete and the squad are so close-minded!" I lament. "If they're staying full-size and protecting the fairy garden, what does it matter if the royal court shrinks? I wish I were the head of the Dwarf Police Squad. If I were in charge, things would be different!"

The bag on Maxine's arm begins to glow.

"What's going on with my lamp?" Maxine asks, but the bag stops glowing before she can open the sack. "Maybe the chemicals are finally working their magic." Her smile widens. The bag glows again slightly, then fades again.

"There's no time to worry about your lamp," I say, grabbing some tablecloths. "We have to get this party ready, whether the royal court comes or not."

We decorate the tables with flower arrangements from the garden. The fireflies finally show up, and the chef promises to deliver a few dozen cinnamon rolls before dessert. We do it all without help from anyone but Ollie, who takes to his new position as self-proclaimed RLW captain quite well.

"I want two more arrangements of hydrangeas on that table, a pink runner on the ground at the entrance, and a line of people with confetti ready to shower our guests of honor as they emerge from their fairy hut," Ollie instructs. "Did anyone think of presenting them with a gift from FTRS?"

Maxine covers her mouth with her hand and looks at AG sheepishly. "No! I was so overwhelmed getting ready…"

"It's okay," says AG, putting a hand on her friend's shoulder. "I'll run back to my pop-up castle and find something we can give." She smirks. "Mother and Father got so many gifts when we moved to Enchantasia, we couldn't use them all so they're just sitting in a closet. I'm sure there's something we can regift." Her cheeks redden. "I know that's wrong, but…"

"It's fine," I assure her. "Go quick!" AG runs off, holding up her powder-blue gown as she races back to the entrance to the fairy garden. She drinks a potion, and *pop!* She disappears, and I know she's full-size again somewhere on the other side of that hedge.

Pop! Pop! Pop! RLWs and students start showing up, with Rapunzel in tow.

"All weapons can go in this sack," Rapunzel says. RLWs begin dropping daggers, wands, swords, bows and arrows, and spell books in her bag as they walk in. "I'll be guarding these all night, so you know what to do if the need arises."

"Maybe we should hang near you, just in case," says Tessa, one hand still on her dagger. "I'm not sure I want to be outside school without my weapon."

"Me neither," says Raza, as her hand holding her slingshot hovers over the bag. She finally lets it drop, and the rest of the RLWs start talking at once. We hear another pop, and Harlow and Headmistress Flora arrive with Blackbeard, his mirror that holds Madame Cleo, and Professor Wolfington.

"Well, it would have been decent of them to at least give us a few hours' notice," I hear the Evil Queen say.

"I know, but under the circumstances, who can predict these things?" Flora says wearily. "If we had known, of course, we would have postponed, but…"

"Aye!" agrees Blackbeard, holding up the mirror so Madame Cleo can look around. "But we be here, so no need to let the grub go to waste." He pats his round belly with his free hand. "Where be the food, boy?" he yells to Ollie.

"We're waiting until the guests of honor arrive before serving food," Ollie says and looks at the other RLWs. "We could use some help with that." They're so busy talking to Rapunzel, they don't answer.

"Honestly, this was a foolish idea with everything else we have going on!" Harlow complains.

"Yes, well, we still need to have normal functions to keep the parents happy," Flora tells her.

"If I might interject," says Professor Wolfington. The four of them fall into a heated discussion, and I get a bad feeling. I glance at Maxine. She's busy rearranging a group of flowers on the head table, so I'm hopeful she can't hear what's going on.

"Maxine!" AG comes running over with a beautiful

jewelry box. "Good news: I found this. Bad news: My parents said the royal court isn't coming!"

"What?" Maxine cries. "No!"

"Why not?" asks Rapunzel, hurrying over with the other RLWs close behind. "Did someone spot Stiltskin?" She dumps the bag of weapons onto the ground before AG can answer. RLWs scramble to grab their weapons.

"Calm down! Nothing has happened!" Even Harlow sounds exasperated.

"But it could!" Flora points out. "Pete got a tip, so the royal court called an emergency meeting. You should probably get going."

"Pete? We're all trusting Pete?" I cry.

Pop! Pop! Pop! Jax, Jack, and Jocelyn arrive. There's no sign of Kayla and her mother yet, but they're supposed to stay in their fairy hut till we announce them.

"The party is off!" Harlow tells the students who have just shrunken down to enter the garden. "Everyone back to their dorm rooms till we get a briefing from the Dwarf Police Squad." She sweeps her gray cape behind her and heads back to the garden entrance with several dozen students in tow.

"No!" Maxine cries, throwing a bouquet of flowers onto

the ground. "I worked so hard! The party was going to be beautiful!" She bursts into tears and runs off.

"Maxine!" I yell, taking off after her. I look back at Jax and the others. "I'll get her."

It takes me a few minutes to finally catch up. I find her sitting on a rock by a waterfall that empties into a beautiful lagoon. She's still crying. I walk over quietly and give her my handkerchief. She blows her nose loudly.

"I worked so hard, you know?" Maxine says, her voice shaky. "AG and I planned everything! And what for? The party is canceled! It's not even as if we're under attack. They just got a tip. *A tip!* And everything is ruined!"

"A tip from Pete, no less." I snort. "As if that guy could find Rumpelstiltskin or Alva. He's a terrible chief! I'd make a much better chief." I sit next to her, pushing her sack aside, and feeling equally glum.

"I know!" Maxine sniffs. "All anyone thinks about anymore is villains attacking! I just wish… I just wish…" The sack next to her starts to glow.

"I wish Pete weren't police chief, that's what I wish," I say. "I wish I were in charge. Parties wouldn't be canceled on a hunch. I'd make a great police chief!"

"I know!" Maxine agrees. "I wish you were police chief too. You know what else I wish?" She pulls her lamp out of her bag. That polish she made must have been really strong because the lamp is no longer tarnished. It's gold and it's glowing. "Look! It worked!" Maxine cries, hugging the lamp to her chest. "At least one thing worked out today." She looks the lamp over and frowns. "There's still one mark right here." She licks her thumb and begins to rub it.

The lamp begins to glow again, and I stare at it in wonder as it turns red from the heat. Maxine drops it as the cap shakes violently and pops off.

"Maxine!" I begin backing up. "What did you do?"

"I don't know!" Maxine jumps off the rock and stands beside me as sparks begin to shoot out of the lamp.

"Run!" I shout, but I'm cut off by the sound of an explosion, a burst of light, and a gust of wind so fierce that it sends Maxine and me flying through the air.

CHAPTER 7

At Your Service

I can't control my body as it spirals toward the lake at rocket speed. I brace for impact, throwing my arms in front of my face, and hear someone shouting.

"That won't do! Stop right there!"

I freeze inches from the water, my arms and legs flat out in front of me. Maxine is suspended the same way. Before I can ask what's going on, we're flown backward at warp speed and placed back on the mossy rock.

"What in the name of Grimm just happened?" I ask, looking around to see who was talking. There is no one at the lake but us.

"Look at the lamp!" Maxine points to the object tipped on its side in the dirt.

A gray puff of steam is emerging from its spout like a teakettle about to boil. I blink and realize it's not actually steam. It's a shape. No—it's a figure—no—it's a—*genie?*

Yes, a genie is spiraling out of the lamp like a tornado. The shape gets bigger and bigger until it's the size of a human. A woman, to be exact, with red curly hair, a gray complexion, and a face full of makeup. I didn't know genies wore makeup. Actually, I didn't know genies were real either. This one sees Maxine, bats her long eyelashes in surprise, and flies over to us.

"Sorry about almost sending you for a swim, Master! It's hard to see what's going on from inside the lamp, you know?" She bows to Maxine. "Darlene the Genie, at your service!"

"Wait, 'Master'?" I repeat. "Maxine is your master?"

"Of course, she is! She's the lamp's owner, isn't she? She talked about wishes and rubbed the lamp, so here I am!" She lifts her right hand, which is ghostly pale and almost see-through, and pats Maxine's arm. "You're dry though, so it all worked out! Sometimes when the lamp is capped for several hundred years, it tends to blow big-time, which causes a bit of a ruckus." She lets out a high-pitched laugh and slaps us both on the back, making us fly forward. "Oops!"

Maxine picks herself up out of the mud. I do the same.

"Did you say I'm your master?" Maxine asks, frowning slightly. "I don't think I feel comfortable being anyone's master. I hate bullies and..."

"Bullies?" The genie's face darkens. "Who said anything about bullying? I'm a strong, independent genie, and I grant wishes. I don't take commands. There's a huge difference! This is supposed to be fun!" She smiles. "You'll get the hang of it. I'll go over all the rules before you make your first wish." She whips a scroll out of nowhere. It keeps unfurling until it reaches the water's edge.

"Wish? I really get to make a wish?" Maxine wipes the mud off her uniform and smiles at me. "I told you magic lamps are real!"

"Of course, they're real! They've been around for thousands of years," the genie says. "I'm only nine hundred and twenty-two, but I don't look a day older than twenty, do I?" She gives us her side profile and puckers her lips. "I do a lot of workouts in the lamp. Spinning is tough without actual legs, but my arms are killer!" She flexes her muscles. "When you have so much free time, how can you not be healthy?" She rubs her hands together. "So, about that first wish..."

"Darlene, I...don't know. I'm not sure what I'd even wish for," Maxine admits.

"Of course, you do!" Darlene insists, throwing her hands up. She takes a hard look at her nails. "Wow, I really need to get a manicure." She produces a file from thin air and begins to shape her nails while she continues talking. "You've read the contract, I take it, so it's not that hard to come up with an appropriate wish."

"This contract?" I ask, starting to roll up the bottom. "No, she hasn't had a chance to read it. You just gave it to her."

"Oh, I'll explain it, dear!" Darlene says. "Basically, the gist is this: You get three wishes. No more. No less. Everyone must take their three wishes, or I don't get to go back to my lamp and relax, and I love my lamp. I just did a complete reno, and the hot tub is to die for."

"Okay, I think I can do that." Maxine's tongue is sticking out of her mouth as she concentrates on the directions. "Should I be writing this down?"

"Nah, it's easy!" Darlene says. "The next thing you need to know are the wish rules: You cannot wish to switch places with anyone, or switch bodies, you can't bring people back from the dead, you can't kill anyone—who's evil—and you can't wish to be a villain. I forbid it. That rule is my personal one, but it's important."

"Fair enough," I agree. "What else does she need to know?"

"No backsies," Darlene says. "Once I grant a wish, I can't take it back. No refunds, no returns. You get what you get, and you don't get upset. The only way to change a wish is make another one that's better. And you can't wish for more wishes either! Understood?"

"I think I have it." Maxine picks up the lamp. "I just don't know what to wish for. I have all these ideas, but how do I know I'm making the right wish?"

The genie stretches out on the rock and stares up at the sun. "No clue, doll face. I'm no therapist. And I love a good musical as much as the next person, but I don't sing for my masters or write songs about wish making. The wish decision is all on you! Let me know when you're ready. I'll wait. I haven't seen the sun in ages! My skin has gotten ghostly pale." She hums a song to herself.

Maxine looks at me in alarm. "I don't know what I want. I mean, sure, a nice big redwood for my parents' new home would be lovely, but Father is already scouting one out. I have all the jewelry I need, and I love our school, and my friends. I don't need anything," she laments. "What would you wish for?"

"I told you," I joke. "To be police chief and have a lifetime supply of patty-cakes. But this isn't about what makes me happy. It's about what would make *you* happy."

"Happy," Maxine repeats.

Just then, two RLWs walk by the lake wailing so loud, I'm surprised they don't wake the hibernating bears. They don't seem to notice Maxine, Darlene, and me.

"I can't believe we aren't under attack by Rumpelstiltskin!" says one. "I really wanted to try some of those self-defense moves Rapunzel taught us."

"I know!" says the other. "Forget about the party. I just wanted to battle a villain and win! Who can think about schoolwork or napkin folding when Stiltskin and Alva are on the loose?"

They disappear through the trees.

"I can't believe they're crying over not getting the chance to do battle!" I laugh. "What has happened to the RLWs?"

"They're obsessed with Stiltskin, battles, and winning this villain war, and can't think of anything else," Maxine laments. "All anyone around here does is frown and complain! I just wish…" Her eyes widen. "I've got it!" She looks at the genie. "Darlene, I have my first wish!"

"What is it?" I ask nervously. Maxine may have the best intentions, but Darlene's warning has me worried. What if her wish doesn't go according to plan? "Maxine?" She runs off, ignoring me. "Why don't you tell me your wish first? Maxine?"

Darlene stretches her arms and yawns when she sees Maxine running toward her. Then she snaps to full attention, her energy back in full force. "Oh goody!" She rubs her hands together. "What do you have for me, peaches?"

Maxine grins toothily. "I wish…" She looks at me. "I wish… I wish for everyone at Fairy Tale Reform School to be happy!"

"Wait!" I cry, but I'm too late.

Darlene folds her arms, closes her eyes, mumbles something, and then there is a gust of wind and a flash of light. "Wish granted!" she announces.

CHAPTER 8

A Whole New World

For a moment, I think everything's gone black. Then I realize my eyes are just squeezed shut. I open them and look around.

"The wish didn't work," I say, looking at Maxine and Darlene. "Things look exactly the same."

Darlene looks indignant. "Of course, the wish worked!"

Maxine bites her lip. "But the forest looks the same. The castle way off in the distance looks the same." She touches her body to make sure it's all there. "Gilly and I are the same."

Darlene rolls her eyes and pulls out a small handheld mirror. She begins fluffing her curly hair. "Think about your wish again, honey. You asked to be *happy*. You didn't ask to be someone else, did you?" She eyes me. "And neither did she. Sort of."

"Me?" I squeak, and Wilson pokes his head of my pocket

to see what's going on. "I didn't make a wish, and I don't want to be part of Maxine's! I do not need things getting any more messed up than they already are. You didn't see what happened with a beanstalk and the giants and…"

Poof! A large platter of gooey snacks appears in front of me.

"Ooh! Patty-cakes. They look delicious!" I take a bite of one, tasting the mix of cinnamon, vanilla, and butter that runs through the delicious confections. Maxine and Darlene are staring at me. "Oh. I guess I did wish for these."

"See? Happy!" Darlene tells Maxine and yawns. "Now, if you don't mind, this air is making my skin terribly dry. I really should get a good hydration mask on before I start to flake. You do not want to see a flaky genie! Especially since I'm going to be meeting so many people through my new master!" She grabs Maxine's hands. "We should have a party!"

"Yes!" Maxine says and then her face falls. "Except no one around here is really in the partying mood."

"Oh, sweetie, you just watch how that changes." She pushes Maxine toward me. "Now, scoot back to the castle and holler for ol' Darlene here when you're ready for your next wish, or when it's time to party."

Maxine frowns harder. "You mean you aren't going to hang

out with me all the time? I thought you'd want to see where we go to school and meet our professors and Headmistress Flora."

"I will, I will!" Darlene says, but she's already whooshing back into her lamp. "But you may want to tell them about me before I go gliding down the halls. I'm sure they'll be thrilled." The lid magically settles back on the lamp, but Darlene is still talking. "Everyone is happy now!"

I grunt. "I doubt that." My patty-cake platter fills up again, and I take another one. "Although, if we give them treats, how can they not be happy and have fun?" I drop the treat on the floor in surprise. "Holy harpies, why did I just say something so sickeningly sweet?"

Maxine giggles. "Because you're happy! Oh my goodness, it worked! Thanks, Darlene!" The lamp lid rattles, and we hear mumbling.

Maxine grabs my hand. "Come on, let's see what's changed at school!"

* ✷ *

When we get back to the castle, our first clue that things have changed is that every entrance is wide open. Lately, the doors have been locked, but now students and staff are streaming out of the building on Pegasi and magic carpets and are... singing? Wait, is that Jocelyn?

A girl that looks a lot like the Evil Queen's younger sister is skipping toward us with a flower in her hair. "La, la, la, la," I hear her sing—*sing!*—as she twirls and dances—*dances!*—her way over to us. "There you two are! We've been looking everywhere! Kayla, I've found them!"

Then she reaches out and does something truly bizarre—she hugs me.

"When we didn't see you at the party, we were worried you got lost," Jocelyn says.

"Party? We didn't have a party," I remind her, and Kayla looks at me strangely.

"Of course, we did, silly!" Her wings are fluttering softly, and she's wearing a ring of flowers in her hair. "Maxine planned the whole thing. My family loved it!"

Maxine smiles. "They did? I mean, of course, they did! I'm so glad everyone had a good time."

"We did," says Jocelyn. "Harlow said we haven't had such a good time since...since..."

"Our last battle?" I supplement.

They both laugh. "Battle?" Jocelyn repeats. "We haven't one of those in ages!"

They grab our arms and yank us inside the castle.

"Come on!" Kayla says. "There's a sing-along starting in the cafeteria, and we don't want to miss it."

When we get indoors, I almost don't believe my eyes. Everywhere I look, pixies are throwing rose petals all over the floor. Students are telling jokes, laughing, or singing songs. And Miri is calling out announcements in the sweetest voice I've ever heard her use.

"Welcome back to Fairy Tale Reform School!" she says cheerily. "The headmistress would like to keep the merriment going and let everyone have the rest of the afternoon off, which means—no classes!"

"No school! No school!" Kids shout and jump up and down.

Hans Christian Anderson, I think the last time Headmistress Flora gave us off from classes, there was a leak in Madame Cleo's tank.

"Can't think of something fun to do?" Miri continues. "Consider joining Blackbeard for a tour of his pirate ship and become an honorary pirate! Or go for a swim in Madame Cleo's tank and meet some seahorses! Professor Wolfington is giving extra credit to anyone who comes by his history class this afternoon. Turn your D into a C! Or drop in on Professor Harlow who's running a basket-weaving class in her lair."

"Basket weaving?" I repeat. "Harlow?"

Jocelyn gives me a look. "Oh, Gilly, you know my sister loves to basket weave. It's her favorite way to de-stress!" Her dark eyes widen. "Did you want to go? I've been meaning to make a new hamper for my room."

"Uh...I think I'll pass," I say as a group of elves with mops come dancing by.

"Gilly! Maxine! Hi!" Ollie shouts as he runs in our direction. "Want to go become honorary pirates with Jax, Jack, and me?"

Jax and Jack together? The two boys, who normally can't stand each other, are walking arm in arm down the hallway.

"Hey, ladies!" Jack says. "First we're going to pick dandelions for all the teachers. They're in full bloom and gorgeous!"

"We'll get you some, if you like," Jax says. "Raz wants us to pick them for everyone. She says there's nothing nicer than a vase of flowers in your room."

"Rapunzel wants everyone to have flowers?" I repeat. "I thought she wanted everyone to live and breathe training."

"Training? What training?" Jax asks. "She's already planning our next party. She says we should have them once a week. Maybe twice." He points to Maxine. "She's looking for you to discuss it. She says you did such a great job with the garden party that you and AG should definitely chair the next party too."

"Really?" Maxine is beside herself. "I don't even know what to say. Flowers in every dorm room and weekly parties!" She winks at me. "I am so happy that everyone is happy."

Jack hits Jax in the arm. "The flowers! We need vases! We don't have enough!"

"That's all right," Jax tells him. "When we're done picking flowers, we'll go to the art lab and make some pottery. It could take us all night, but it will be worth it."

"You're right!" Jack agrees. "You're a good friend."

"No, you are!" Jax tells Jack, and then the two do some strange secret handshake I've never seen either of them do before. Then they head off.

Zap! Zip! Bang! Boom!

I duck as someone's wand action sends sparks in my direction. I look up. It's Headmistress Flora. Suddenly the wall that appears behind me is a shimmery green. A swath of flowers cascades from the ceiling above me like a canopy, and a trio of songbirds in a beautiful gold cage hangs above our heads. The birds chirp in harmony.

"Hello, girls!" Headmistress Flora says. Her hair is pulled back, as usual, but the bun is looser, as is her dress, which is a lovely shade of yellow that matches the flowers around her neck. I try not to laugh at the sight of our prim headmistress loosening up. "What do you think of the birds? Too much?"

"Um, they're kind of loud," I say as one bird hits a high note.

"Yes, that could be distracting in class." She zaps her wand again, and they disappear. "If we even have class this week! The weather is supposed to be gorgeous, so Harlow, Wolfington, and I think you should enjoy the outdoors as much as possible. We've been cooped up for too long."

Maxine nudges me. "Have we? Why do you think that is?" she prods.

Flora thinks for a moment. "Well, I… Oh my, I don't even know! I guess it's been too chilly out, but it's unseasonably warm, and the flowers are blooming so we should take advantage of the beauty Enchantasia affords us! And we should bring that beauty inside too." She waves her wand again, and a fountain with a cherub appears. "I'm trying to spruce up the place," she tells us. "Castle décor can be so dour, and Fairy Tale

Reform School is anything but!" She zaps the wall again, and a beautiful painting of mermaids frolicking in a lake appears. I suddenly realize all posters warning of Rumpelstiltskin attacks are gone. "We should have fine art and music in the hallways, and lovely carpeting beneath our feet." She conjures a beautiful orange rug into existence, but it disappears when a new wall appears. "Maybe we should change how we get around school too. How do you feel about slides?" She thinks for a moment and smiles. "Or trampolines?"

"I love trampolines!" Maxine exclaims, and they both start talking.

"Trampolines?" I interrupt, unable to believe what I'm hearing. "In the hallways? And slides?" I start waving my arms wildly, feeling annoyed. "I just can't believe…ooh! A patty-cake!" One appears in each of my hands, and I take a bite before I realize what I'm doing.

Wait a minute… Every time I start to get the least bit unhappy, my favorite snack appears. I growl at Maxine. This is her wish's fault! Two more patty-cakes appear.

I give up.

"I'm supposed to meet with Professor Sebastian this afternoon," I tell Headmistress Flora. "Have you seen him?"

"Why, no! He wasn't at the party. He must be enjoying his afternoon off in his pop-up castle," Flora says with a smile so peppy, I fear she's an imposter. "Why don't you take a flying carpet to go visit him? Have a lovely time!" A pixie flying by blows glitter in all of our faces. "Oh, how sweet! Thank you!"

A lovely time? With Professor Sebastian? I doubt it, but for the first time ever, I think I'd prefer his company to anyone else's at school.

Happily Ever After Scrolls
Brought to you by FairyWeb—
Enchantasia's Number One News Source!

Unusual Happenings in Enchantasia

by Padreig Parsnip

Villagers and farmers alike have appealed to the royal court and the Enchantasia Dwarf Police Squad to get to the bottom of the strange weather that has occurred the last few days. "There has been lightning and thunder on sunny days!" Farmer Bob of

Illensville told *HEAS*. "I've never seen anything like it, but it's been causing crops to catch fire, and we lost our barn from it." High winds have been blamed for knocking down one of the three little pigs' abodes as well (although, witnesses say the house was made out of twigs, for what it's worth). Investigators have ruled out the possibility of a wolf culprit.

In addition to the weather, several farmers have reported a strange goo-like substance covering their crops. "It's green and sticky and sometimes smells like peppermints," Penelope Ward told *HEAS*. "It eats away at the radishes before they're fully grown. I fear I've lost my whole crop this year."

Matthew Goodie, chief Enchantasia weather expert, said the weather and the goo could be related to one creature. "Legend has it the typhira, a small, goblin-like beast that preys on crops and schoolchildren, can also affect the weather. If one is on the loose in Enchantasia, we should all stay locked inside till it moves on to a new kingdom. They are almost impossible to catch and could burn you with one touch. Do not engage with one. You won't win."

"Those things are a myth!" said Goodie's nemesis and author of *Real vs. Myth? The Creatures We (Actually) Should Be Worried About*, Jeff Doshler. "No one has ever found proof that typhiras really exist. How can an animal control the weather?"

"I object to Doshler's objection," countered Goodie. "Does he have proof that the animals are indeed not real? Until he does, I urge all citizens to take caution during storms. And cover your crops!"

The royal court told *HEAS* that it is looking into the matter, while appeals to the Dwarf Police Squad have remained unanswered. "Pete is buried under paperwork and will respond as soon as he can," says a squad spokesperson.

Stay tuned for details on the unusual happenings in Enchantasia.

CHAPTER 9

A Fairy-ly Important Discovery

I find Blue waiting for me outside the castle like an eager puppy. I'm not sure if magic carpets can be put under spells or if Blue is just his usual lively self, but he whisks me off past the vegetable gardens and the pumpkin patch, past a group of mermaids singing siren's songs in the lake, and over a game of leap frog in the garden.

I don't think I've seen people this happy since…ever!

When I arrive at Professor Sebastian and Beauty's castle, I'm not surprised to find more of the same attitude. I find AG spinning around the room in a pink party dress, arms stretched wide. Her brown curls twirl around her face, making her look almost like her half-beastly self.

"Gilly!" AG cries. "Come spin with me!"

"No, thanks," I start to say, but AG grabs me, and we go round and round. She giggles repeatedly as we stare at one another, going faster and faster.

Obviously, AG has been affected by the wish too.

My head is spinning after just two twirls.

"What the devil is going on?" barks Professor Sebastian. We stop, and I watch him descend the steps, passing portraits of himself, Beauty, and AG that decorate the staircase. Several of the staff hear him coming and take off.

"Father! Hi!" AG says. "Look at us, we're spinning!"

AG gives a hard yank, and the two of us go flying across the room, landing on a velvet couch. AG is doubled over laughing, but I'm staring at Professor Sebastian. He's dressed in a red velvet jacket with gold buttons and black dress pants. I look down at my muddy uniform and wonder what he's going to say about my appearance. I didn't have time to change. I had to get out of school.

He growls at us, and I've never been more happy because this means he hasn't been affected by the curse!

He looks at his daughter. Then he looks at me. "What's wrong with her?"

"Well," I start to say. "A wish was made with a genie in

a magic lamp, and I think AG—and the entire school—has been affected."

Professor Sebastian slaps his head. "Who did this?"

I hesitate to call out Maxine. "I don't know," I lie.

He narrows his eyes at me. "You seem the same."

"I overheard the wish being granted, so maybe it doesn't affect me the same way it does the others." His nostrils flare. "I think? Where is Beauty?"

"She's in the village buying books," he says. "I suspect she's been spared like you, but Allison Grace…"

AG shoots up off the couch and begins to bounce. "You know what would be fun? A stroll through the forest! It's such a beautiful day, and I really would like a chance to stretch my legs a bit and get in some exercise." She closes her eyes, starts to breath quickly, and hair rapidly begins growing all over her body. She's transforming before our eyes!

"Allison Grace, what on earth are you doing?" Professor Sebastian asks.

"Embracing my beastly side! I told you I wasn't embarrassed anymore! Now I can run free and—*hoowwll*!" She drops to all fours, her party dress starting to tear, and takes off out the open front doors.

I smile as she retreats. I really hope this development isn't wish related. I love her newfound confidence. Think of all she can do in the Hollow Woods without worrying about her beastly side! She could be a real asset out there in beast form. "Good for her!"

I realize I said that part out loud. I look over at Professor Sebastian.

He doesn't look as happy as I am about this development.

"You're late," he says, walking away. I suspect I'm meant to follow.

"Yes, well, as you can imagine, with the wish, people are acting a little strange. It was hard getting down the hallways with all the confetti, pixie dust, and balloons. There are even fireworks planned for tonight."

He turns and looks at me. "Fireworks?"

"Yes." I nod. "Professor Harlow's idea."

He runs a hand through his long hair, which is pulled back in a low ponytail. "Fairy be, what a mess. Well, at least you've kept your wits about you." He pulls open a doorway at the end of the hall, and I see a beautiful library full of bookshelves that reach all the way to the ceiling. A large stained glass window lets in a kaleidoscope of colored light, which filters over a stack of books sitting on a large desk. He motions for me to take a seat.

"I thought it was time we had that talk I promised."

I sink into a large armchair with satin cushions and try to contain all the questions I'm dying to ask. I know better than to blurt them out. He'll just get annoyed. I lean forward expectantly.

He sits across from me, puts on a pair of spectacles, and opens books to various marked pages. I watch and wait. Professor Sebastian opens his mouth wide and prepares to speak.

"How would you like your tea?" he asks.

Tea? I don't want tea—I want to talk! I bite my lip. I know what he'll say. Tea is needed for a proper, civilized conversation. I exhale slightly. "With a lump of sugar, please."

He nods, pleased. "Now, Gillian, I know you have many questions about Rumpelstiltskin, and how the two of us crossed paths, but I am not going to tell you that story today. Truthfully, it's not as important as everything else we have to contend with."

Oh fiddlesticks! "I thought you were going to tell me everything!"

"What happened to me is in the past," he insists. "What's

going on with you is the present—and our future. Right now, it's more important that you and I concentrate on this fairy book about Stiltskin's history." His blue eyes are thoughtful. "Sadly, I don't know much about its content. I cannot touch the book...unlike you."

"How do you know that?" I ask.

"Information like that can't be ignored," he says. "Professor Harlow told me straightaway. As you know, the only person who can open that book is the fairy who wrote it *or* someone with fairy blood. Yet, you're human." He cocks his head. "Or are you?"

"I am human," I say. "Both my parents are human, and my grandparents are human..."

"So they tell you," he says, scratching his chin. "Where are your grandparents from?"

"Mother's parents live on a farm outside the kingdom," I tell him. "Father's father is no longer around, and we don't see my grandmother Pearl."

He raises an eyebrow and sort of grunts. "What do you know about Pearl?"

"Nothing! I've never met her," I say. "Father and Grandmother Pearl don't get along, but his father was a shoemaker like he is. My family has been making shoes in Enchantasia for over sixty years between Father, and my grandfather, and his father. Everyone loves our glass slippers. Or they did before Princess Ella's fairy godmother started conjuring them." I roll my eyes. "But now Princess Ella lets Father make them again, and it takes almost a week to make a pair so it's a real pain, but they're popular and… I don't remember your question."

Professor Sebastian smiles. "Where do you think your family got the idea for such a creation? Glass slippers are fairy shoe originals, passed down from one fairy to another. If the Cobblers know how to make them, then they were likely given that knowledge by a fairy. Possibly a fairy in their own bloodline. Maybe your great-grandparents. Have you ever thought to ask?"

"No," I scoff. "Because I don't have wings." If we had fairy blood, wouldn't Mother and Father brag about being magical? I can't recall magic ever being used in our house or at Grandma's in the woods. I think hard. Has anyone ever mentioned fairies other than in talking about my former roommate, Kayla? "I think you're wrong about this."

He smiles, enjoying himself. "I think I'm right. And to

prove it, I'm going to give you an assignment. I want you to write to your parents about this."

Not more homework!

"It's okay. I don't need to know either way," I start to say.

"Yes, you do!" Professor Sebastian insists. "There is a reason you were able to pick up that fairy book and a reason you were able to make the harp come to life in Cloud City. I'm sure of it! And if I can figure it out, then you can be sure Alva and Stiltskin are going to figure it out soon too and come looking for you."

"Why would they look for me when they have Anna?" I ask quietly. "If I have fairy blood, then she does too."

"True," he agrees. "She did make the harp work with you, which would lead me to guess that two fairies in the same bloodline are better than one for the magic they're looking for. And if that's true, and they realize it, they'll want you on their side more than ever before."

"So I'm doomed?" I ask worriedly.

"Not at all! Your true love for your sister made that harp come alive," he explains. "While she had ulterior motives, your heart was pure. And in times of war, that can make all the difference. Good always wins in the end, but it can use some help getting there. If you can hold that book, you can help Angelina protect it until she's done writing it. Think of it as being a police chief for the most important book in the kingdom." He winks.

I don't share his enthusiasm. "What good is holding that book going to do? Even if we know how Stiltskin's story ends, we are no closer to figuring out how to stop him. And now with everyone being so distracted with this wish, he could easily catch us off guard! What if he's casting his curse as we speak?"

"He's not," Professor Sebastian says knowingly. "He doesn't have what he needs to cast the curse yet, and he's no closer to finding the ingredients to cast it."

"How do you know that?" I snap, growing grumpy. *Poof!* Patty-cakes appear on the desk between us.

Professor Sebastian raises his right eyebrow but doesn't question their appearance. "I've always wanted to try a patty-cake. May I?"

"Be my guest," I say with a sigh. "The sight of them is starting to make me ill."

"Hmm, quite sweet. I can see how they'd be appealing." He takes a few bites, then blots his mouth and puts the rest down. "Want to know why I believe Stiltskin is stalled? And scared?" He looks like a kid lording information.

"How?" I ask.

Professor Sebastian pulls out a wand, and *poof*! A new book appears. I jump out of my chair in surprise. It's Angelina's fairy book about Rumpelstiltskin!

"How? Why? When?" I start to question.

"I am letting him borrow it with my help to read it," says Angelina, appearing out of the shadows of a bookcase. Kayla's mom looks well rested and not at all crazed like she did when we last met in the forest that night. She's wearing a flowy, blue gown that sparkles against her bright yellow hair. "Don't be frightened of it," she tells me as her wings flutter softly. "I brought it here so you could both read it. There are few I trust to explore its contents, but I agree with Professor Sebastian. You have a connection to this story too now, Gillian. You tricked him once. You made him believe you had the golden egg. You came close to saving your sister…"

"And failed," I finish.

"You were tricked yourself," Angelina argues. "I came here today so we could share some knowledge. I don't know much yet, I admit. I have only just written the battle you fought in Cloud City, but I do know if Alva is awake, she isn't at full strength. Not even close. And Rumpelstiltskin has no clue what ingredients he needs to cast a curse as ambitious as yours." She smiles. "What I'm saying is, time is on our side. We don't have to act rash out of fear. We can figure things out."

"That's good," I agree. "Because people aren't themselves right now."

Angelina laughs. "Oh, I heard about the wish. Even Kayla is affected. But I was here, so I guess I, too, am immune." She pushes the book toward me. "Why don't you take a little time reading what I've written so far?"

I stare at the book in front of me. Read about what happened in Cloud City again? What Anna did to me? I close my eyes tight. I'm not sure I could bear it. Maybe it will help, or maybe it will hurt more. "No, I don't think I want to…yet."

Angelina and Professor Sebastian look at each other. "Okay," she says. "We won't force you. For now, why don't you concentrate on finding out your family history. It would be better for you to know now, before your sister figures it out herself. We can always meet again soon. Maybe then you'll be ready."

"Maybe," I say. "Thank you for trusting me," I add. I know Professor Sebastian always expects us to be polite.

Angelina wands the book toward her, and she disappears into thin air.

Professor Sebastian looks at me with interest. "You're free to go, but you still have to do your homework."

I groan. I'm about to complain when the doors to his chamber burst open. AG is back in human form, and she has Maxine with her.

"Guess what?" Maxine cries, her face flush. "It was just announced! Fairy Tale Reform School is putting on a musical!"

CHAPTER 10

Auditions!

A Fairy Tale Reform School musical?

Is the sky falling?

Over the next few days, everywhere I turn, people are singing or practicing big, passionate speeches for their auditions. There are signs offering "macting mentoring" from Professor Harlow of all people, who has agreed to critique students' performances before their actual audition. I went to see Kayla do hers for the fun of it. I expected Harlow to snap out of it and give a droll, deadpan analysis of Kayla's rendition of "Three Blind Mice." Instead, the Evil Queen swatted away a tear at the end of Kayla's performance!

"Gilly!" Ollie runs after me, ducking to squeeze through a closing hallway. "Ready for the audition? I'm going to sing a pirate sea chantey. I've been warming up all morning." He hums a few notes. "What do you think?"

"Not half bad," I admit. "Ollie, you really *want* to be in the musical?"

He looks affronted. "Of course! I have a chance to sing on stage with a group of mermaids watching me adoringly. How can I not take it? Even Jax is going to sing something. He was in a musical at Royal Academy."

"So I've heard," I say dryly, pulling my books closer to my chest as I squeeze through a closing doorway.

Jax has been bragging about his macting work at Royal Academy for days. He's been offering people tips and everything.

"I'm going to paint the displays," says Jocelyn, joining us. I do a double take. Today she's wearing a canary-yellow, silk dress with an embroidered FTRS crest on her chest. I suspect she made this herself, but I can't find it within myself to ask. Jocelyn does not sew! She does not wear color! Enchantasia has gone batty!

I growl, and *poof*! A plate of patty-cakes appears in front of me.

"Oooh, patty-cakes!" Ollie exclaims. He and Jocelyn

each take one. A group of kids gather round, and I motion for them to clear the plate, which keeps refilling.

Patty-cakes are great, but after your eighth or ninth one in a week they tend to lose their appeal. Just the smell of one now is enough to make me gag.

"Gilly, are you okay?" AG is carrying three large scripts. One has a beanstalk drawn on it.

"I'll be fine," I say and eye her material. "What is that?"

AG flashes us a shy smile. "Musicals, of course! Jack wrote them."

"Jack wrote a musical?" I repeat.

AG nods. "It's really good! He's made copies for all the teachers in the hopes they'll consider doing a musical based on his life, instead of Madame Cleo's *An Ode to Enchantasia*. What is hers even about?"

"I know! She's being so secretive," Jocelyn agrees. "Harlow and Madame Cleo have been working on it the last few days, but they want the story to be a surprise. Cleo says it's a love letter to the kingdom." Whereas normally Jocelyn would snicker at this, she sighs and grins. "I think it's beautiful of her to want to do that."

"It is," AG agrees, "but Jack's story is a true survival tale that would appeal to everyone at FTRS. At the auditions, he's going to recite from his own musical—titled *Jack and the Beanstalk*—and I said I'd perform with him. Kind of like a duet."

Quack! Peaches pokes her head out of Maxine's book bag.

That seems unwise, considering how Peaches likes to eat everything from fruit to pocket watches, but Maxine says Peaches acts as good protection for the lamp. I wouldn't want to wrestle that lamp away from Peaches, I'll tell you that.

"It's nice of Jack to ask you to perform with him. I hate having to audition alone." Maxine casts her eyes downward, and one eye rolls in its socket nervously.

"You don't have to!" AG swishes back and forth excitedly. "There's a third important part if you want it." She bites her lip. "It's the part of the cow. I don't know if you would want to play a talking cow, but the cow has the best dialogue in the musical. Really riveting moos and such."

"Maybe I will be the cow," Maxine says, and I pull her aside as AG continues telling the others about the magical cow in Jack's brilliant musical.

"You do not have to be the cow," I whisper. "This whole musical is your idea! You should get to be the star."

Maxine shakes her head. "It doesn't work that way. Yes, I

wanted everyone to be happy, but I didn't know happy meant a school musical! I'm excited everyone is excited, but I don't know if I can do this show. I'm not a performer." She gazes at the ceiling in a daze. "I want to wear a beautiful gown and sing on stage while my mother and father watch proudly from the audience…but that's not going to happen." She looks at me blankly. "I have a terrible voice."

"No, you don't," I say before realizing I've never actually heard Maxine sing. "Do you?"

Maxine nods tearfully, then pulls me into a doorway. She starts to sing "Do You Know the Muffin Man?" in a high, off-key voice. I quickly cover my ears, but a bird in an open window isn't as lucky. It screeches in terror and flies off as two glass vases shatter. I hear people in the hallway shouting in bewilderment. ("What is that? An alarm?")

"See?" Maxine throws her hands up. "I wish I had a beautiful voice so I could star in the musical!"

At the word *wish*, the lamp in her bag begins to rattle and shake, and the cap pops off. A gray haze fizzes out of the spout and takes the shape of Darlene. The genie is wearing a sleep mask, bright pink polka-dot pajamas, and is talking into a seashell. She doesn't seem to notice us.

"Uh-huh. I agree! I was just telling Betsy that a trip to the snow caps would be miserable this time of year. We're better off going somewhere warm to celebrate her birthday. I need an excuse to wear this new floral dress I just got shipped to the lamp. Not wear a snow jacket and boots!" She stops talking and sniffs the air. Then she removes her sleep mask and blinks. "Jeanine, I've got to go. My master is here with her second wish." She nods to the shell. "I know. I know. Hopefully the third one will come faster than the second. We have a birthday bash to plan!" She laughs. "Okay. Talk soon. Bye-e!" She looks at Maxine and flashes a dazzling smile. "Hello, darling! It's wish time! Yay!"

"I didn't make a wish," Maxine insists. "Did I?"

"I distinctly heard the word *wish*," Darlene says. She snaps her fingers, and a mirror appears in her hand. She fluffs her hair and puts on earrings, then changes into a red gown. "Ah, much better for wish granting." She looks at Maxine. "So you want a good voice and the lead in the musical so that everyone will adore you, right? Easy!"

"Yes, that does sound nice, especially if I knew how to dance as well, but—" Maxine starts to say.

Darlene closes her eyes, says a few words, and there is a

gust of wind. "Done! You now have a beautiful voice and a penchant for dancing!"

"I do?" Maxine clutches her chest.

"Try it! What were you just singing so terribly? I could hear you in the lamp," Darlene says, making a face. "Try again."

Maxine begins "Do You Know the Muffin Man?" a second time, and this time she sounds lovely. She's definitely an alto, but her voice is smooth, strong, and melodic. Maxine is usually a klutz, but Wish Maxine is twirling and spinning and pulling off moves I've never seen before. Both Darlene and I are entranced. When she's finished, we can't help but clap. Maxine's gap-toothed grin is priceless. She's so proud, and she should be. Even if, well, it's not really her voice or moves. But we're the only ones who know that.

"My work here is done!" Darlene begins to put her sleep mask back on. "Call me soon about that third wish."

"No!" Maxine cries. "I'm not making a third wish!"

"What?" Darlene asks. We both look at her.

"It's just, my third wish shouldn't be so selfish," Maxine realizes. "I want my third wish to be important and help the kingdom. Something to stop Rumpelstiltskin."

"I don't know," I say warily. "A wish like that could be risky. Look what happened with your first wish."

"I know." Maxine nods fervently. "Which is why I won't take this wish lightly. I'm going to wait however long it takes till I think of the right wish, Darlene. You should get comfortable because you could be here a while."

Darlene throws her eye mask down in a huff. "But I hate to be bored! Absolutely hate it! And with the lamp being grounded at FTRS, I can't go to my genie conference this weekend or plan Betsy's birthday trip. I have a busy life, you know. I don't just grant wishes."

"I can see that," says Maxine. "And I'm sorry, but I can't be foolish. I'm happy everyone is happy, and I'm excited about my singing voice and the fact I can dance now, but the third wish has to be really thought out." She snaps her fingers. "But if you're bored, why don't you help with the musical? You're obviously very stylish and have a lot of ideas. Maybe you could direct it."

"I think Harlow's the director," I whisper.

"Or choreograph, do the scenery and help assistant direct." Maxine is getting really passionate now. "There is so much we need help with."

Darlene clutches her long, dangling gold necklace. "Well, I wouldn't want the musical to be a disaster, especially after my wish inspired it." She looks at me. "What would the other genies think if it was a flop?" She squares her shoulders. "All right. I will help with the musical!" Maxine claps excitedly. "We should go talk to this Harlow you mentioned."

"The Evil Queen," Maxine explains, leading the way. Darlene floats along after her. "Well, she's not really evil anymore, but it's hard to distance yourself from a nickname like that."

I start to follow them into the hallway when I hear a noise. "Psst!"

I look around. No one is there.

"Psst!" A white-gloved hand appears from around an adjacent doorway and beckons me to come closer. I am so surprised, I follow and find Princess Ella in a bright-pink ball gown standing in our school hallway without an entourage or the police squad.

"Thank goodness I found you, Gillian!" she exclaims. "I didn't know who else to call. Everyone here has gone mad. Rapunzel hasn't returned to discuss security details, and my stepmother is concerned about some school musical. What is going on here?"

I sigh. "I know. It's a bit of a mess." But I can't really say Maxine made a wish. If word got out that everyone associated with Fairy Tale Reform School was under an enchantment, who knows who could come after us? What if Rumpelstiltskin found out? No, it's better not to tell the princess. This way she stays safe. "I guess everyone needed a break from battles and war talk, so they're doing a musical. Written by Madame Cleo." She can't be buying this.

"That's splendid, but we can't forget our battle plans! We don't know when Stiltskin will attack or try to curse the kingdom or get Alva back on her feet again. This is not the time for a musical!"

I've never heard Ella this worried. I don't blame her—I'd be pretty worked up if I were the one in charge, but at least she has the rest of the royal court to help. Well, minus Rapunzel, who's under the enchantment as well. And Rose, who isn't really in a position to help at the moment. (Plus, I don't trust her.) But, um, she has Snow, right?

"I don't know what to do," Ella cries. "Pete is talking about leaving town and taking…" she pauses, "…a vacation!"

"A vacation? Pete?" Ella must have heard him wrong.

"Yes, things are falling apart! With Pete gone, no one at

the Dwarf Squad knows what they should be doing or how to handle security issues. You know, we've been having an issue in the east part of the kingdom with some sort of creatures attacking crops. No one can catch it, and now the problem seems to be spreading across the countryside. I'm worried they'll reach the village soon. What if they're dangerous? I don't know what to do without Pete around."

"I'm so sorry." Maxine has to fix this. "I'm sure things will go back to normal soon."

Ella nods. "Please try to talk some sense into my step-mother, will you? And Rapunzel? They both listen to you. You're a smart girl, and you've done so much to help the kingdom. I know you can get through to them."

I clutch my chest. Wow. That's huge coming from Princess Ella. "I'll try," I promise.

With a wave goodbye, she slips back into the shadows and sneaks out of the castle, which I'm really impressed with because I didn't know she had that sort of cloak-and-dagger move in her. I go to the window and watch her take off on a Pegasus just as another one lands with a very short man on top of it. A man that looks really familiar.

"Pete?" I ask as he comes running toward me, *smiling*.

"Gilly! My girl!" He hugs my legs. "Just the one I wanted to see!" He rips his police chief badge off his vest and, before I even know what's happening, pins it to my uniform.

"What are you doing?" I cry.

"Giving you a job!" he says with glee. "I'm going on vacation, and I'm leaving you in charge!"

"Me? Why me? I'm just a kid!" I tell him, astounded.

"You said you could do my job better than I could, didn't you?" Pete asks. "Well, now you get the chance! I need a break from this Stiltskin stuff, the beanstalks, the trolls and ogres fighting, and the security concerns at this school, not to mention the new problems with whatever unknown creature is ruining farm crops and attacking villages. One torched a thatched roof in Enchantasia and…" He shudders. "Well, it's not my problem anymore. It's yours! Have fun!"

"Pete, wait!" My heart is pounding. "I can't leave school. I still have classes with Professor Sebastian and my fencing club, and I'm not ready for a full-time job yet."

"You can do it!" Pete insists.

I'm in a total panic now. "You said a former thief can't be police chief!"

"I'm changing the rules!" Pete says and heads back to

the Pegasus. "You'll be fine. You can work from school. I'm sure Professor Sebastian and Headmistress Flora won't mind. Everyone thinks you can save the kingdom! About time you actually did!" He laughs. "You said being Dwarf Police Chief would make you happy, right?"

My face drops. No, it can't be. Maxine's wish. I growl.

Poof! Patty-cakes float in a bowl in front of me.

"Oooh, patty-cakes, send them my way," Pete says.

I hand over the whole batch.

"Thanks." He puts one in his mouth. "Great travel food. Have fun. Any questions, well, just wing it."

Then he takes off into the sky, leaving me wondering what I've gotten myself into.

Pegasus Postal Service

Flying Letters Since the Troll War!

FROM: Gillian Cobbler (Fairy Tale Reform School)

TO: Mrs. Cobbler (2 Boot Way)

TOP SECRET! FOR INTENDED'S EYES ONLY!

Mother,

All is fine here at school—I promise! No need for me to come home, although you may see me soon. I got a school job! Kind of. Pete, the Dwarf Police Squad Chief, is taking a vacation for the first time ever and has put me in charge while he's gone. Headmistress Flora thinks it's a great idea for my Magical Metamorphosis development. I get a shiny badge and everything! I haven't had much to do yet, but everyone is congratulating me. Oh, and I'm also playing a tree in the school macting musical. (No need to come. I have one line.)

I wanted to ask you something, but you can't tell Father. I know how upset he gets when this comes up, but since you mentioned her in your last post: What can you tell me about Father's mother, Grandma Pearl?

Love,
Gilly

CHAPTER 11

A Star Is Born

ᴧ ttention, everyone! Attention!" Madame Cleo's voice
is piped into the room for all land-based students
while several mermaid students float around her, reading
scripts from waterproof paper Professor Harlow conjured
up. I watch as Cleo's tail swishes back and forth turning
green, then red, then yellow. "Would everyone please get
into position?"

People move every which way at once, and I find myself
and my tree costume getting spun around as a troll wearing a
red wig runs by me carrying a giant sunburst. Jack is dressed
like an actual beanstalk, and AG looks like her everyday self
in a peach ball gown that has an overlay of lace on the skirt.
Jax takes her arm, and I notice he too is wearing peach and

a white wig. The two of them won the parts of the musical's narrators.

"Isn't this so much fun?" Jax asks me. "I love your…er, tree costume." He touches one of the papier-mâché leaves that someone has glued to one of my twigs. "What is your line again?"

"He's over yonder!" I repeat. The rest of the time I stand in the background perfectly still. Or I sneak offstage to eat a patty-cake, which is always waiting for me since this musical business makes me really cranky. I begged to be part of the stage crew, or even paint backdrops, but Headmistress Flora and Professor Harlow said: "Your face shines too bright to be hidden in the background." Whatever that means.

"Brilliant," says Jax, sounding way too serious for my liking. "This musical is the best thing that ever happened to Fairy Tale Reform School."

"Isn't it?" AG asks.

They both have a dreamy, far-off look on their faces. If only I could snap them out of this wish-fulfilled daze. That's not a bad idea… Maybe a good knock will wake them up. I find myself swinging my tree branches and "accidentally" hitting them both in the stomach.

"Ouf!" cries Jax. "Gilly, what are you…?" I swing around again. "Ow!"

"Ouch!" AG clutches the beads on her corseted waist. "That hurt! I feel…"

"Yes?" I say hopefully, leaning my entire tree trunk and branches forward to listen. Say something feels off! Say you're mad at me! Say you want to know why I just did that! Just say *something*. After one week of Maxine's dreamy "We're all happy at Fairy Tale Reform School" world, I've gotten sick of morning sing-alongs on the way to class, smiles on everyone's faces, and a devil-may-care attitude about the little trickster and the wicked fairy who are plotting our demise while we rehearse *An Ode to Enchantasia*.

But instead of reacting the way I'd hoped, both AG and Jax smile again.

"Accidents happen," AG says.

"No one was hurt," Jax agrees. "We should get to our positions though. We're running the whole show today. Break a leg, Gilly!"

Kayla appears out of nowhere. "You're not supposed to say that, remember?" she whispers. "It offends the mermaids since they don't have legs."

"Oh." Jax's frown lasts a mere moment. "May magic be with you, Gilly!"

Kayla beams. "This show is going to be wonderful, don't you think? Well, I better get backstage." She's the unofficial backstage director. Kayla likes giving orders. She consults her clipboard. "Harlow said we were doing the pirate scene first… Ollie, where are you?"

"Argh!" Ollie runs at me with a sword aimed at my tree trunk. He stops short in front of us and grins. "How was that? I'm a pretty convincing nasty pirate king, if I do say so myself." He's got an eye patch, a red bandanna, a leather pirate vest, and leather boots, all of which came from his own closet.

"Let's go over your backstory again," Kayla says. "You are Pirate King Loran, the greatest pirate Enchantasia has ever seen." She's reading from an official playbook that has Harlow and Madame Cleo's notes all over it. Apparently, they wrote the entire script over dinner the day Maxine made her wish. "You have defeated all the villains there ever were, and you are afraid of nothing because you are happy! Living in Enchantasia means never fearing what comes next."

Ollie salutes her. "Got it! I am a happy pirate king! How can I not be?" He looks at me. "Enchantasia is the best place ever!"

I'm going to be ill.

"Yes, but maybe we should tweak the dialogue just a bit." I struggle to move my tree limbs to reach Kayla's script. I point at the lines in question with one of my leafy hands. "Defeated all the villains ever… That's not true, is it? Rumpelstiltskin and Alva are still out there, and we should be preparing for their attack." They look at me.

"That's your job," Kayla says simply, and Ollie nods. "You're police chief. Besides, we're safe here!"

"Yes, but I'm just one person," I try again. "I'm not saying we should live in fear, but FTRS has always tried to be prepared for any situation. We can't pretend there isn't a villain after us when there is, can we?"

"Oh, Gillian!" Headmistress Flora says as she walks by with a bouquet of flowers. "We're fine! We're safe here! No use worrying about what won't happen, now is there?"

"Yes, but what if…" I start to say.

Harlow approaches, laughing. "Oh, such a worrier, you are, Ms. Cobbler. With myself and the other professors here, there's nothing to fear. Relax! Be happy!" She holds up a mega-phone and shouts to Madame Cleo, who is choreographing a mermaid dance number. "Ready to run the show?"

Flora cranes her neck. "Yes. I'm not sure where our assistant director is though."

Kayla consults her clipboard. "She had a manicure scheduled this morning followed by a deep-tissue massage that ran long, but she should be here soon." She looks at me. "Planning a musical can be so stressful."

"She'll be proud we started without her. Let's begin!" Madame Cleo claps her hands with delight. "Places! For real this time." The cramped room, which was never meant to be used for a theater production, is quiet except for the *drip, drip, dripping* of water overflowing from Cleo's tank. "And we're on!"

The mermaids in the tank begin their dance, doing synchronized swim moves alongside some eager puffer fish. Blackbeard stares at Madame Cleo with pride as he hums along to the tune the Pied Piper is performing as our introduction.

"You're on!" Kayla whispers, and Jax and AG come out arm in arm to stand center tank. Er, I mean, stage. A group of pixies rush to the stage and fly around them.

I reluctantly go and stand in the corner next to a team of ogre sunbursts and a group of fairies playing, well, fairies. Wilson pops his little head out from a hole in my tree trunk and begins chittering loudly. He's as annoyed as I am about this whole musical business, but I shush him before we get in trouble.

"Enchantasia has always been a fair kingdom, known for its beloved royal court and its kind and gentle citizens," Jax begins. A group of students "ooh" in harmony on Madame Cleo's command.

"So beloved are they, that others flocked to this land to make it their own, much like my family," AG adds, smiling. I glance at Harlow and Cleo who are mouthing all the lines alongside Jax and AG.

"Villains may darken our doorstep, but they cannot dampen our day," adds Jax, as Jack, dressed as a beanstalk, twirls by. "We are too strong for them! Sunshine always bursts through the clouds on a rainy day, just like we do!"

"Um, that's not necessarily true," I say to those around me. Wilson chitters in agreement.

"Shh!" says the ogre dressed as a sunflower standing next to me.

"For Enchantasia has never turned its back on any creature, big or small, winged, or one-eyed. All who dare to dream are welcome—even ogres," AG says, and motions to the sides of the stage.

Everyone turns and stares at Maxine as she walks stoically onto the stage in a sparkly blue gown that makes her look like a giant cupcake. She begins to sing. "Oh, Enchantasia, the land we call our own. Enchantasia! We adore thee! We wouldn't be anything without thee!"

The sunflower next to me sniffs. "She has the voice of an angel."

"A *flock* of angels," argues the sunflower next to her.

I hear sobbing and turn around. Tessa and Raza are openly crying.

"Could there be a better star of this show?" Tessa wonders aloud, dabbing at her eyes with a handkerchief. "She acts, she sings, she can dance like a true star. She's unbelievable."

"How have we not known how talented she was?" Raza asks, blowing her nose loudly.

Both girls are understudies, which is funny because Tessa has a great voice, and I was sure she would get the lead, but… then Maxine cast her second wish. Now her voice is like that of a canary's—high and melodic…and not real. I bite my lip and try not to say anything. If I do, patty-cakes will appear.

When Maxine finishes singing, the entire room breaks into a round of applause.

"Encore! Encore!" Raza shouts, and Maxine curtsies.

"That was lovely, Maxine," Harlow says. "But Cleo and I were thinking that maybe during the second stanza you could—"

The doors to the room fly open, and Darlene floats in wearing a spa robe. Her hair is wrapped in a towel. "The assistant director has arrived." Everyone stops what they're doing and bursts into wild applause. Darlene makes the moment even bigger by shooting a few indoor fireworks, which make the mermaids in Cleo's tank swim away in panic.

I notice Harlow's right eye twitch, and I feel a flutter of hope. Maybe, just maybe, she's starting to break out of the wish spell!

"What's this? Did you start without me?" Darlene casts a critical eye on the stage setup. "We need bigger lighting! A grander stage, maybe a bigger tank for the mermaids."

"That would be lovely!" Cleo begins, and Harlow frowns. "And Darlene, darling, we need better lighting for Maxine. I want everyone's eyes in the room on her, especially on opening night when the royal court and the entire village is invited to attend."

"The entire village?" I repeat. "And the royal court? That doesn't seem safe, plus I feel like it might be a fire hazard in these cramped quarters."

Darlene scratches her head. "True. We need a bigger venue." Her eyes widen. "Maybe the air? I'm thinking magic carpets for seating. Pegasi flying around and offering drinks and snacks."

"Everyone likes snacks," Blackbeard agrees as he munches on a turkey leg.

"Outside?" I cry. My heart is pounding harder. I think of Ella's warning. I have to get people to see reason. "I don't think that's a good idea. Anyone could attack." I look at Maxine, who is suddenly staring at the rafters.

"Oh, Gillian," Headmistress Flora dismisses me. "You're such a worrywart. We'll be fine! We have you, don't we?"

Now I see why Pete was always harried and lost all his hair. People don't listen to the facts! When people get complacent, disaster—a.k.a villainy—happens.

I stomp over to Maxine. "You need to put a stop to this," I growl.

Maxine nods up and down, drool spilling out of her mouth. "I know. And I will! Soon!"

"How soon?" I ask as a patty-cake platter floats between us.

She bites her lip and pulls on her gown. "Like in another two weeks? After the run of the musical is over?"

"Maxine!" I scold.

"I can't give up this chance to perform, Gilly!" Maxine cries. "My whole family is coming! Mother and Father are so proud. So are my grandparents. They didn't know I could sing."

"Because you can't!" I hiss. "We can't afford to go another few weeks like this. What if Stiltskin is ready to strike again?"

She scoffs. "No one has even heard from him or seen him. You've said so yourself. We have more to worry about with this year's crops and the typhiras. I really hope one shows up here. They're so cute!"

"They're not real!" I run a hand through my hair, and it gets stuck on a tree branch. I yank and pull out a few strands. Ouch. "I need to focus on the real creature doing this. Some creature is eating crops and attacking farms, and I need to figure out what it is. Plus, I got an alert about a freak storm near the edge of the Hollow Woods. One lightning strike could burn down the forest, and then the giants would have nowhere to camp out and could run out of the woods and trample the school…" I sigh. My head hurts thinking about every possible thing that could go wrong. "Look, we have to be more careful. We can't just hope no one will attack us."

Maxine sets her jaw. "And we can't live our whole lives

in fear either! We deserve to have some fun! And sing! And perform!"

"You have to fix this wish!" I insist.

"After the musical opens!" Maxine shouts back.

"Before!" I thunder.

"Ladies?" Darlene floats between us. "This is not the time nor the place for a conversation like this. Maxine is our star, and trees do not upset our star."

"Darlene," I beg. "Don't you want your job here to be done? Aren't you ready to get back to your newly renovated lamp?" Her expression falters. "Convince Maxine to make her third wish and you can be home! Forget the musical."

"But I like the musical," Darlene admits, pulling the towel off her head and revealing super-bouncy pink curls. She's had her hair dyed! "I'm enjoying directing. Who knew I could have so much say in things? I never get a say in wish granting. I think Maxine should make her third wish after the musical run is over."

I growl angrily. *Pop! Pop! Pop!* Suddenly two trays of patty-cakes appear, and the pile of snacks on top of them continues to multiply till the tray almost reaches the top of Cleo's tank.

"Ooh! Snacks!" Ollie shouts, and people come running. I get separated from Darlene and Maxine in the chaos and feel something pulling on my arm.

"Gilly! Gilly!" a girl shouts. "There's been an attack! Someone's at the castle doorsteps looking for the police chief."

"So?" I start to say, then remember. That's me.

CHAPTER 12

Paging Chief Cobbler

This is the first time I've been called on at school to be acting Dwarf Police Chief. I need to be professional.

"So tell me exactly what happened," I say to the girl who sent for me. I try to use my best serious voice. I should really have a scroll on me and a quill. Does Pete take notes? Should I already have called for backup? I fire off a series of questions to the girl who is stuck playing messenger: "Have you spotted a creature at our doors? Is it a recognizable villain? Or a giant attack? I've recently learned giants can be friendly, but one can never be sure who they're crossing paths with. What kind of attack was it?"

We reach the foyer. A group of dwarves are arguing. The

girl stops and looks at me strangely. "They said it was an attack on vegetables."

Vegetables? That doesn't sound like a very pressing matter for the police chief.

"I told you to stay off my farm!" one dwarf yells, throwing his right arm back and hitting the other dwarves in the face with goo. They're all covered in a strange green slime. They're so busy arguing, they don't realize we're there.

"Well, I'll leave you to it," the girl says. "I need to get back for the theater break. The genie meet-and-greet is today. Don't want to miss it."

"Genie meet-and-greet?" I repeat.

"Yes." The girl pulls a pink quill out of her uniform dress pocket. "I'm fifteenth in line, and my friend Rita is holding my spot. Darlene's going to sign our scripts and do a story time about some of her former masters. She's even going to provide snacks." She sighs. "Everyone loves her."

Snacks. Like Maxine, I don't think Darlene is ready for her stay at Fairy Tale Reform School to be over. She's clearly enjoying the attention after not having any for a few hundred years. No wonder she's stopped pushing Maxine to make her final wish.

"You threw first! Not me!" another dwarf shouts.

"Can you blame me? You ruined three bushels of my crop with your stunt!" says a third dwarf.

"I told you I didn't do it!" says the first.

I can't tell what this vegetable problem is with all the yelling. "Gentlemen?" I try. They keep yelling. "Sirs?" Nothing. I put two fingers in my mouth and whistle. *That* gets their attention. They all look at me. "What seems to be the problem?"

"Who are you?" demands a dwarf with green slime all over his face and in his beard.

"Yeah, where is Pete?" asks another. "We asked for the Dwarf Police *Chief.*"

"You're just a girl...dressed as a tree," says the third.

"Pete is on vacation." My face warms slightly. "I'm, uh, filling in."

"They put a kid in charge of kingdom security?" The first blots his face with a handkerchief. "No wonder things are such a mess."

"Would you rather speak with Headmistress Flora?" I ask hopefully. "Or Rapunzel? She's a member of the royal court, and both are on school grounds."

"They said to ask for you," sighs one of the dwarves.

"Didn't know you'd be a kid though." They all mumble in agreement.

I exhale sharply. "Are you going to tell me what happened? If not, I have musical rehearsal to get back to." Which suddenly sounds way more appealing than dealing with these guys.

"See this all over me?" asks a dwarf with slime all over his blue overalls. "He threw this at my farm! Now my entire crop is ruined!"

"Why would I do that, Hank?" asks the second dwarf, sounding clearly exasperated as he removes his green spectacles. "I grow vegetables too, and my crop is also destroyed! Now no one near Fawn Lake can get a fresh radish if they want one!"

My ears perk up. "Did you say radish?"

"No one anywhere in the kingdom can get their hands on a radish," corrects the third dwarf, who has the longest white beard I've ever seen. "There are no radishes anywhere! Or gingerroot! Or strawberries!"

"Just those three fruits and vegetables are ruined?" I ask, feeling confused. Why would anyone ruin a radish crop? Radishes are great for getting rid of those nasty gargoyles. The hair on my neck stands up. Could the gargoyles have taken them all? They were Alva's spies. But I haven't heard of any sightings. The headquarters have been sending me daily scrolls with crime reports, and the only thing I've seen is some lady rambling about a typhira. People couldn't get them confused with gargoyles, could they? "Did you see anything flying over your property? A gargoyle, perhaps?"

"If a gargoyle was on my farm, I'd know," sniffs the first dwarf. "I know people claim they saw a typhira, but we all know there's no such thing. This was a prank. And they started it!"

I rub my temples the best I can with these leafy arms. How can Pete deal with these issues on a daily basis? I can handle a dragon on the loose or a beanstalk on school grounds, but people arguing over vegetables… I just don't think I have the strength. "So this prank involved covering both your crops *and* each other in goo?"

"No," says Hank sheepishly. "The radishes are missing. The goo is on the remaining crops. We just have it on us because we threw it at one another. The only crops I have that aren't ruined are blueberries."

"All I have are my green beans," says the third dwarf. "This has been happening for weeks. We keep appealing to headquarters to send someone out, but every time they do, there is nothing going on. The attacks happen at night. Maybe you could camp out and watch for yourself?"

"I'm not allowed to leave school at night without permission," I tell them. Plus, I'm not sure I'd want to camp out to see who is ruining radishes. It's not like anyone was hurt. "But I will send some squad members out to take samples of this slime and look for clues." I pause. "And you're sure you haven't seen any flying gargoyles?"

"No!" Hank shouts. "Gargoyles don't frequent these parts." He looks at me suspiciously. "Aren't you supposed to be the police chief? You should know that." The other two snicker.

My face feels hot. "I know. I'm just checking."

"Then check on the weather too," says the second dwarf. "It cannot be sunny and warm one moment and then snowy the next. It doesn't make sense."

He's right, it doesn't. According to Ollie, typhira can change the weather. But they aren't real, are they? Something isn't adding up. "I will send someone out to investigate as soon as I can. We're also trying to track down Rumpelstiltskin so resources are slim."

Earl's eyes widen. "Slim? This is our livelihoods at stake! Come on, fellas. This kid doesn't know what she's doing."

"This kid?" I cry, and *poof*! More patty-cakes appear. The dwarves eye them eagerly. "Here. Take them as a parting gift," I say wearily.

Hank snatches the tray of treats and walks out the door. "As if patty-cakes could make up for my radishes," I hear him say. "Ooh! These are good though."

"Gilly, there you are!" Miri the Magic Mirror lights up behind me; the mirror's glass is a mix of blue, yellow, and pink swirling colors. "I've been looking for you. I have a Dwarf Police Squad update," she says cheerily. "Red says there was an incident at Red's Ready-for-Anything Shoppe with a customer refusing to pay for the protection charms they wanted to buy. They broke a broom in anger on their way out the door. Two Pegasus coaches collided in the village square, toppling an apple cart and causing damage to Pinocchio's puppet theater. The Enchantasia Civic Association has requested a meeting to discuss ongoing lake revitalization efforts and a possible new mermaid-under-the-sea shop that someone would like to open. Two more farmers have made accusations about, well, each other, regarding their strawberry fields, which are covered with green goo."

"Is that all?" I slide down against the cold, stone wall and onto the floor. I have a massive headache, and I've just realized it's going to be awfully hard to stand back up in this tree costume.

"Nope! Margaret Hamlet of 2 West Wind Way says her door was vandalized by children who should be in Fairy Tale Reform School but aren't because, and I quote, 'It seems like Fairy Tale Reform School is too busy chasing villains to look after the youth anymore.' And there have been two more typhira sightings, if you believe that sort of hogwash." She snickers. "If I were you, I'd ask Pete to come back from vacation ASAP." Her mirror fades to black.

She's annoying, but she's not wrong.

"Gilly!" A fairy races around the corner and spots me on the ground. She flies over me. "I've been looking everywhere for you!"

Oh no. Not another problem. "Yes?"

"Maxine needs you to come to the Creature Care classroom right away. Peaches is eating everything in sight!"

Peaches is always eating everything in sight. Is this really a job for the Dwarf Police Chief? Maybe this is what Pete meant when he said this job wasn't just about battling villains. Maybe it really is about making every person who comes to you with a problem feel like they've been heard. I can't clamp Peaches's mouth closed, but I can be there when Maxine needs me. "Can you help me up?"

The fairy pulls me up and whisks me through two hallways before depositing me in front of the battered Creature Care classroom doors. They're closed, but I can hear the symphony of neighs, chirps, and elephant roars from here. I quickly enter the room and find cages rattling, animals running around, and a llama standing on a table.

"Maxine?" I call.

"Back here!" I spot her outside the back door of the classroom in the paddock where creatures like AG's unicorn Butterscotch, are kept. She's still in her full costume and makeup. "Come quick!"

I run back and find her locked in a tug of war with Peaches over a radish.

"Help! She's going to eat it!" Maxine cries, tugging on the radish.

I'm confused, but I rush over, pulling on the back of Maxine's arm as she tugs the radish from Peaches's mouth. I'm trying to remember if Peaches is allergic to radishes and if that's why Maxine is so upset. But I don't think Peaches is allergic to anything.

Peaches has her beak clamped down hard on the radish leaf roots. We give a valiant effort, but man, is Peaches strong, and it seems like the other animals in the room are watching and cheering her on. Jax's dog is yipping, Ollie's parrot is squawking, and the llama is pawing at the table nervously. Actually, a lot of the animals seem nervous. Is it because of Maxine's blue wig?

"Pull!" I try one more time, but Peaches yanks harder, and we go flying, hitting the floor.

"Stop her!" Maxine cries, but it's too late.

Peaches swallows the radish whole and lets out a massive burp. The other animals only make more of a ruckus.

"Why can't Peaches have radishes?" I ask breathlessly.

"She can, but she shouldn't because that's the last of the radishes at school," Maxine says, her left eye rolling around in the socket. "I was in the middle of singing my big number before intermission, and Peaches started squawking about some radish shortage and not wanting *them* to get ahold of them. Something about 'save the radishes!' which didn't make sense to me so I kept singing, but then Peaches took off and all these animals burst into Madame Cleo's room in terror, and Peaches was gone, so I ran here and found her eating every radish in sight while the other animals cowered in their cages in a panic." She lifts a sticky shoe. "And there's all this goo over the floor."

"How would Peaches eating all of the radishes save them?" I ask.

Maxine blinks. "You know Peaches. She likes to protect things. And she said you weren't doing a good job so it was up to her." We both look at Peaches.

Peaches glares at me. *Quack!*

Even Peaches thinks I'm not cutting it.

The animals continue to shake and cower, with one cat meowing loudly and a corral of chicks peeping madly. They're clearly upset about something.

"When you came in, did you see anyone else in here?" I ask, and Maxine shakes her head. I look at Peaches. "Was it a gargoyle?" I try. That causes mass hysteria. Peaches is flapping her wings and going wild. "You *did* see a gargoyle?" I ask again.

"No! She said no!" Maxine snaps. "No one saw anything. Peaches said she just came to save the radishes. Which she did. But I really wish she hadn't eaten all of them. It isn't nice to be greedy, Peaches," Maxine scolds.

Peaches burps again.

I look around the room for clues, checking the troughs.

The only things missing are strawberries and radishes. Gargoyles don't like strawberries, do they? Do typhiras? *No! Don't be ridiculous, Gilly. They're not real!*

"I need to get back to rehearsal, and Darlene wants to go over some new promotional scrolls so..." Maxine starts to back out of the room.

"Maxine, this is getting out of control," I tell her again.

"I know, I know," Maxine says again, looking forlorn. "Just give me another week until the musical. Please, Gilly? I need this."

I look at Maxine's pleading face and cave. It's just some missing radishes. It's not a beanstalk in the vegetable garden or a dragon in the school gym. I sigh. "Okay. One more week."

Pegasus Postal Service

Flying Letters Since the Troll War!

FROM: Gillian Cobbler (Fairy Tale Reform School)

TO: Pete, Police Dwarf Squad (Address Unknown)

PETE! WHERE ARE YOU?

I can't do this! I don't know how to be a Dwarf Police Chief! I'm a kid, and every time people bring me another

---

problem, I realize more and more I don't know how to fix things. I'm trying, but—and I can't believe I'm saying this—I need your help. Please come back! Immediately!

Sincerely and with much regret,

Gillian Cobbler

RETURN TO SENDER:
FORWARDING ADDRESS
UNKNOWN

CHAPTER 13

The Show Must Go On

"Good morning, Fairy Tale Reform School!" Miri the Magic Mirror's voice radiates in our room. "Please note all classes are canceled today so students can concentrate on what's most important: our first ever musical!"

Cheers can be heard throughout the dorm tower. I bite my lip and look at Wilson. We seem to be the only two not excited about this. Maxine has been up since before the sun, fixing her few locks of hair with curlers, which Peaches keeps eating. Darlene has been meditating in her lamp after being up late last night for a pre-opening night party she threw. This is not to be confused with the opening night party that Darlene's throwing after the first performance, or the closing night party, which will take place in two days' time. I've even heard talk of a musical reunion party that she's supposedly throwing a few months from now, but that's impossible because Darlene and her lamp will be long gone by then, right? *Right?*

Whenever I ask Darlene or Maxine that question, neither answers me.

"Due to low enrollment, the school-wide assembly taught by Professor Wolfington, 'Evil Throughout the Ages: How to Identify and Take Down a Villain,' has been replaced by Madame Cleo's 'Don't Worry, Swim Happy' lecture. Madame Cleo's enrollment, on the other hand, is almost full! It will take place next Tuesday."

"Ooh, Peaches, I need to find a good bathing suit to wear to Madame Cleo's lecture," Maxine tells her duck, who quacks. "I know you don't need one, but I do."

"Professor Harlow has announced a cooking tutorial in her dungeon to help students de-stress. She says, and I quote, 'Making food that feeds the soul can help us all be calmer.' Bring an apron and join Harlow for a 'Ways to Cook with Apples' seminar next Saturday afternoon."

Wilson pokes his head out of my pocket and looks at me. "Ways to cook with apples? With the Evil Queen?" I ask my mouse, and we both laugh. I laugh so hard, I fall on my bed, which is covered with scrolls sent over from police headquarters. They send scrolls for everything. If a single spoon goes missing at Three Little Pigs restaurant, there is a scroll about it.

"I don't think it's funny," Maxine sniffs. "I think it's great that Harlow is putting her, er, talents to good use."

"She's tried to poison people with fruit before," I remind Maxine. "I'm not sure she should be teaching apple recipes. She should be using her magic to track down Stiltskin!"

Darlene's lamp uncorks, and she emerges from the smoke wearing a sparkling pink face mask. Her hair is in curlers, and she's currently painting her see-through genie nails a bright purple. "Did someone mention that heinous villain's name again? Why are we talking about him? No one has seen him, have they?"

"No!" I start getting worked up again. "But that's just because everyone is bewitched!" I hold up a stack of scrolls. "I'm the only one scouring the news for mentions of that angry little troll! You guys are too busy putting on a school musical!"

"To make people happy," Maxine reminds me.

"They're not really happy!" I shout. "That's an illusion you created with your wish!"

Pop! A sterling silver tray full of patty-cakes appears on my bed. Maxine immediately takes one and starts chewing.

"I love these," she says. "They calm my nerves. Darlene, have one."

"No." She waves them away. "I ate too much at last night's party."

"The roasted chestnuts were really good."

"Weren't they?"

"Enough!" I cry and another patty-cake tray appears. "When are you two going to get your head out of the clouds and cast that final wish? It's time Fairy Tale Reform School gets back to normal."

Maxine and Darlene look at each other in a way I don't like—a way that says they've been talking without me. "What did you two do?"

"It's more like what we *haven't* done," Maxine says sheepishly.

"And what we don't plan on doing," Darlene says, removing the curlers from her hair. She shakes out her red locks, and they fluff up to twice their normal size.

"You're not fixing your wish?" I screech.

Maxine tries to shush me. "We've talked about this a lot, and we sort of don't think it's necessary anymore."

"Everyone is so happy working on the musical," Darlene adds. "Who says they can't continue to be happy? Why do they need to worry about a villain who hasn't made a peep since you last saw him? They have lives to lead."

"Lives that should be happy," Maxine adds.

I can't believe what I'm hearing. "But, you're tricking them into thinking everything is fine when it's not."

"As opposed to them spending every waking minute thinking about a villain who isn't here?" Darlene counters. "Who's to say what's better? Besides, this is the first place I've visited outside my lamp that I actually like. You kids get me, and I love directing." She gets a far-off look in her almost-transparent brown eyes. "I'm already thinking of our next musical: *A Summer in Enchantasia*. We could have singing flowers and fairies flying over the audience dropping snacks."

"Great idea!" Maxine agrees, and Peaches quacks.

"Stay? But you need three wishes! That's the rule! You said so yourself! You wanted Maxine to be done!" I remind her.

Darlene shrugs her nonexistent shoulders. "That was before I got to know you all. And if that Stiltskin is really out there, don't you think my lamp should be with Maxine rather than just waiting to be found? What if it falls into one of his squad member's hands?"

I open my mouth to argue, but it's kind of a good point.

"It could be a total catastrophe," she presses. "Which is why Maxine and I decided she won't cast a final wish. I'll stay with the two of you." She grins. "My new roomies!" My jaw drops. "I hardly take up any room with my lamp, and the staff seems to really like my musical direction. I'm sure they'll love having me full time."

"Aren't you breaking a genie oath or something?" I'm starting to full-blown panic. Fairy Tale Reform School cannot live in a permanent bubble! Professor Harlow is at her best when she's conniving and plotting revenge against people. Madame Cleo loves detention! And none of the students are reforming the way they need to, because they're all living a false version of their lives! I feel like the walls are closing in on me. "What would your fellow genies say?"

Darlene's face clouds over slightly. "Well, they don't have to know, do they?" Maxine and Darlene look at me.

Before I can say anything, Miri is back with another announcement.

"Madame Cleo and Professor Harlow would like all

students to come down to the gym for a dress rehearsal this morning, to be followed by a celebratory lunch before it's time for everyone to get ready for tonight's show," Miri announces.

"Lunch?" Darlene cries. "I didn't know anything about a lunch! How can they throw a lunch when I'm throwing a dinner? That's too much food before a performance. I must speak with them." She goes flying through our dorm room door in a panic.

"Guess we should get ready to go." Maxine gathers all her supplies. "Father and Mother sent a Pegasus Post that they'll be here by three. They're bringing all our neighbors and my grandparents too. I'm so excited!"

"Maxine," I say kindly. "I'm happy for you, but doesn't any of this feel...untrue to you? Don't you want them to come see *you* perform, not as some wished-up version of you?"

Maxine bites her lip, drool dripping off her chin. She doesn't answer me. "Are you coming along?"

"Maxine, please think about this final wish," I beg. "It's dangerous to have it just hanging out there! What if someone tries to force you to make a wish you don't want? Then everyone here will be stuck in this wish-state forever! Fix things before it's too late!" *Pop! Pop! Pop!* More patty-cakes appear on my bed. "Please."

"Gillian?" Miri is back again. Grrr… "The village shop-keeper association would like to talk to you about some vandalism to their shops. You know, you really should hire a secretary. I don't have time to handle your affairs as well as the school's."

"Thank you, Miri," I say sweetly, but by the time I turn around, Maxine is gone.

I don't make it to the dress rehearsal. No one comes looking for me. I guess when you have one line and play a tree, no one notices. The shopkeepers keep me tied up forever.

"Someone is setting fire to our boots and teakettles," one shopkeeper says again. "How else do you explain a burn mark on my teakettle top? It's not like it was a lightning strike. It was a starry night!"

"I did hear a few rumbles of thunder," admits one shopkeeper.

"I'm telling you, it's the typhira!" cries one.

"There's no such thing!" says another.

I hand them all a scroll. "If you would just write down exactly what happened to each of your shops, I can send someone out to see what's going on."

"Why can't you do it yourself?" asks the shopkeeper.

"I am in a musical tonight," I try, my cheeks coloring. "And I'm late for rehearsal." It's a lame excuse for a police chief to use, but I'm desperate.

The shopkeepers start complaining, but get distracted by a bolt of lightning and the sudden pounding of rain against the castle roof.

"But it was supposed to be a clear night!" laments one shopkeeper as he pulls up his hood and heads to the door.

"Better get home before it gets worse," I say, pleased by the sudden weather making them exit. "The Dwarf Police Squad will check on your shops soon." I get them outside to their Pegasus coach then lock the doors behind me. I breathe a sigh of relief.

"It's harder than it looks, isn't it?" someone asks.

I look up and see Professor Wolfington and Professor Sebastian standing together at the end of the hall.

"What is?" I ask, wiping the rain off my face.

"Being a leader," Professor Wolfington says. "Pete may have screwed up sometimes, but he made his job look easy."

"Which, as you now know, it's not," adds Professor Sebastian.

"Are you saying I can't do the job?" I bristle.

"No," Professor Wolfington cuts me off. "We're just pointing out that even with years of training and a lot of patience, this job is difficult." He looks at me kindly.

"But Rumpelstiltskin could be out there right now!" I argue.

"But he's not," Wolfington says gently. "It takes time and resources to plot revenge. He's too busy to come after us. For the moment."

I look at him strangely. "Wait. You're not acting happy. Are you not under the enchantment?"

He chuckles and looks at Professor Sebastian. "Those of us with an inner beast aren't usually affected by wishes."

"And yet somehow, AG has fallen for it wholeheartedly," Professor Sebastian says with a sigh. "She's more human than I realized." He scratches his head. "If I have to hear her sing, 'Oh, Enchantasia,' one more time…"

"Right now, Gillian, the best thing you can do is help Maxine make the right decision about her final wish," Wolfington reminds me. "And to help her make it soon."

"Stiltskin may be plotting, but he won't be plotting forever," Professor Sebastian adds. "Angelina says he's gathering the ingredients he needs for his curse as we speak. And once he has them and Alva returns to full strength…"

"But Maxine won't listen to me," I tell them, feeling sort of hopeless.

"Then try harder," Professor Sebastian says. "A student who wants to be the first reformed-thief police chief should be good at negotiating." He raises his hairy right eyebrow. "Shouldn't she?"

The task is daunting, but then again, I've always liked challenges. I can't help but start to smile. "Yes, she should."

CHAPTER 14

Opening and Closing Night

I grab my tree costume and head down to the gym where everyone is already in performance mode. There are hundreds of chairs set up by the makeshift stage, and a huge curtain separates the performers from the audience. Behind the curtain, I can hear people warming up, a piano being tuned, and shouts of "Has anyone seen my script?" Next to the stage, the mermaids are practicing their synchronized swim moves in a giant tank.

Madame Cleo is directing the students—both inside the tank and out—on where she wants things to go.

"The flowers should be at the entrance, darlings," Madame Cleo tells Blackbeard and a group of pirates. "If anyone wants one to throw at the stage—or a starfish to give to a mermaid—those buckets should be at the door where we'll be collecting tickets. I'm also thinking some flowers along the walkways would be a lovely touch."

"No, no, no, stop right there." Darlene swoops down the aisle. "I don't want any of my performers tripping when they come down the aisles singing, 'How Do You Solve a Problem like Enchantasia?' That is an accident waiting to happen."

Madame Cleo's tail turns a fiery red. "What are you holding in your hand, darling?"

Darlene puts the scrolls behind her back. "Nothing."

"More autograph-signing scrolls?" sniffs Madame Cleo. "Aren't you a little busy to be signing autographs?"

"Yes, well, I am, but when the students beg…" Darlene says.

A crack of lightning lights up Madame Cleo's tank with an eerie glow. Her face is anything but happy, which is interesting. Can a wish's power fade? But she quickly smiles again. "That's lovely, darling, but save it till after the performance! Our guests will be coming soon." Madame Cleo notices me. "Gillian, dear, why are you not in costume yet? We're doing the run-through in ten minutes!"

"I just need to find Maxine," I protest and turn to the genie. "And you too. I—"

Darlene ushers me to the dressing rooms—a.k.a. gym locker rooms. "Dress first, talk after! Bye!" I go flying through the doors.

Inside, it's mayhem.

"Has anyone seen my halo?" Kayla yells as she flies through the room.

"Sparkles! We've run out of sparkles!" shouts a pixie, who is doing hair. A group of girls are lined up waiting for their turn.

"I think this one needs some blush. She looks quite pale," I hear Miri say about a small elfin girl wearing a sunburst costume. "Either that or she's about to…"

Oops. I turn away as the girl throws up into a trash basket. Thankfully, someone from the elf cleaning crew appears with the ELF Cleaning Spray, and one quick spritz later it disappears before it starts to smell.

Everywhere I look, girls are applying stage makeup and getting into elaborate costumes designed as trees, sunbursts, and teakettles. Mermaids in their gym locker tanks are adorning their shell tops with pearls while pixies drape themselves with flowers. AG is dressed like the princess she is.

"Gilly!" She runs toward me in a sparkly beige ball gown with a tulle skirt. "I'm so nervous. This is my first show, and

I've never spoken to this many people before. What if I start to turn beastly?" She looks worried, but then a smile pops back on her face. "But it will be fine either way, because I am happy! Always happy!"

This wish is so strange.

A boom of thunder rattles the windows.

AG frowns again. "I hope this weather doesn't delay the visitors coming to see the show."

Darlene whisks into the room. "Places everyone! We are going to do a run-through and then it will be showtime!" There is a flurry of excitement as everyone stampedes to the door.

I strain my neck trying to find Maxine, but she's nowhere to be seen. I slip into my tree costume and rush to the door. *Poof!* A cloud of sparkle dust makes me start to cough.

"There!" says a tiny pixie. "Your hair has that cool purple stripe, but you didn't style it so it needed some pizazz. What do you think?"

I glance in the mirror. My brown hair is almost entirely pink and covered in sparkles. I look like a giant cupcake dressed as a tree. "Er…"

"Let's go, Gilly!" Darlene says. "Everyone is already on stage!"

"Gilly?" Miri yells for me from a nearby mirror. "The Dwarf Police Squad called. The storm has washed out the bridge to FTRS, and they won't be able to send any backup for the musical tonight. They want to know if you're okay on your own."

"Umm," I say as a group of students dressed as cows pushes past me.

"Has anyone seen the glass slippers?" AG shouts.

"I think my beanstalk costume needs more green paint on it," Jack yells to anyone who will listen.

"Someone took the wrong pink dress!" Jocelyn almost barrels me over. "I'm sure it was a mistake, but I really need the pink dress with the diamond collar!"

"I…" I try to come up with a response, but I'm so distracted by all the shouting and the sparkles flying through the air, I can't concentrate. "It's fine!" I yell over the chaos. "With the weather, I'm sure we'll have a smaller crowd than usual." Rain is pelting the window harder now, and the wind has picked up.

"I'll let them know," Miri says. "They also said to tell you there have been a few disturbances this evening. The first one was—"

"She has to take the stage! It's time!" Darlene pushes me out of the locker room and toward the stage, making me miss the end of Miri's message. Maybe it's about more farmer crop issues? Or more issues caused by the weather? I glance outside. The sky is almost black. Funny, but that shopkeeper was right: I don't remember there being any rain in the forecast.

"Gilly!" Darlene snaps. "Get in position!"

I run to my mark and look around for Maxine. Where is she?

"Our star has arrived!" Tessa points to the audience. Maxine is walking up the aisle flanked by two dozen ogres. They're so large, they knock over a bunch of chairs.

"Mother, Father, this is everyone," Maxine says proudly. "Everyone, this is my ma and pa!" They're both wearing WE LOVE MAXINE T-shirts with an abstract painting of what I think is Maxine on the front.

Everyone yells hello or waves. Darlene coughs loudly, and Maxine makes her way to the stage.

"Psst! Maxine!" I hiss.

"Shh!" the ogre sunflowers around me shush.

Maxine doesn't turn. She's obviously avoiding me. She knows what I'm going to say. I'm sure of it.

"I want to see smiles!" Darlene floats around the stage. "Show off your macting skills! Practice your breathing. In and out. In and out. Exhale slowly."

Everyone does as they're told, jumping at the sound of another clap of thunder.

"Showtime!" Darlene magically opens the giant curtain.

AG steps forward. "*An Ode to Enchantasia*, directed by the brilliant Darlene the Genie, with an assist by writers Madame Cleo and Professor Harlow."

"Cut!" Harlow rushes up the aisle in a pink gown and cape. I'm so shocked at her princess-like outfit, I almost pass out. "An *assist*? Cleo and I wrote that script. Our names should come first. You're the assistant."

Cleo's tail is green with envy. "Darlene, we talked about this. Our names should come before yours. We wrote the script."

They start to bicker, and I wonder if maybe someone has overridden this wish, but then Darlene snaps her fingers and their smiles return.

"But if you want your name first, it can stay that way." Harlow air-kisses Darlene. "Sorry for the interruption."

"Thank you!" Darlene says. "Continue, AG."

"This fair kingdom has been known throughout the land for not only its struggles, but its triumphs."

Jax steps forward, wearing a gold lamé jacket and shiny black pants. Normally, he'd never be caught in a number like that. "With the help of fairy godmother Olivina, the royal court rose to power as a united front, ruling the kingdom of Enchantasia with a kind, but firm hand."

The mermaids in the tank start to dance, and the chorus made up of RLWs starts to sing as Maxine walks to center stage.

"Oh, Enchantasia!" Maxine croons, in her beautiful— fake—voice. A pixie next to me sighs with happiness. "The land we call our own…"

The thunder booms and a flash of lightning illuminates Maxine's face.

"Gilly!" Miri appears in the handheld mirror of the girl next to me. "Gilly! There's been a break-in!"

Did she just say break-in? It's hard to hear over the oohs and aahs…and *screaming*? Is that Miri?

"Gilly! Help!" Miri cries.

"Stop!" I shout, interrupting Maxine's song.

"Gilly, whatever it is can wait," Darlene tells me.

I grab the mirror and rush forward, banging people with

my tree limbs as I race to reach Maxine. "I think Miri is in trouble! We have to stop the show and help her!"

"Gilly!" Jocelyn snaps. "You're being rude and sound jealous! It's not polite to interrupt the show's star."

"I know you only have one line and it makes you sad, but it's not good to lie," says Ollie.

I hear more thunder. The claps come one after another, and the ground starts to shake. Are we under attack? Is it Rumpelstiltskin? I look for someone who appears as alarmed as I am, but the other students are either yelling at me about interrupting the show or humming the musical's melody. Harlow and Cleo look blissful, and Flora is nowhere to be seen. Miri and I are the only ones worried.

"Gilly!" Miri's little mirror turns red. "Get the students to safety! They're here!"

Boom! Seconds later, the doors to the gym blow open.

The strangest creature I've ever seen comes scurrying into the room. With big, pointy ears, and a long, white body that he walks on with all four paws, he reminds me of a dog. He sniffs the ground around him, appearing not to see us.

"Aww, how cute!" says Tessa. "It's a dog. Gilly, you're worried about a dog?" Everyone laughs.

At the sound of so many schoolchildren, the creature looks up and opens its mouth. A lightning bolt shoots out of it, hitting the row of chairs behind Maxine's extended family, setting it ablaze. The ogres begin to run in different directions.

"It's a typhira!" Maxine's father shouts. "Maxine, run!"

For the love of Grimm, those things are real! Maxine was right! Legend says they hate schoolchildren and are mischievous. And we're in a fairy tale reform school. Excellent.

"Aww, they're so cute!" Maxine says as the creature begins to squeak in a high-pitched voice. Maxine looks at me. "Told you they were real! I always wished I could see one in person and now here they are."

Wished. That's right! "Maxine." I grab her by the shoulders. "You were talking about these little devils when you were polishing your lamp!" Her eyes widen, and one begins rolling madly in its socket. "Them being here must have something to do with your wish!"

More typhiras scurry in, fanning out to sniff the ground, climb the walls, and search the room. Spotting the food on the side of the stage, they squeak louder and head right toward it. They knock over anything in their path—overturning tables and chairs to get to the food, and tearing through the platters in a matter of minutes. Plates fly and tablecloths are shredded as the pack fights over every last morsel. When it's all gone, they spot the school kids cowering on stage, and their eyes narrow.

"Everybody, run!" I shout as the group of tiny beasts bare mouths with three rows of pointy teeth. They start to growl and rush toward the stage.

"What's wrong with them?" AG asks pleasantly as one bounds toward her.

I knock her down just in time, and the creature lands behind us, opening its mouth.

"Roll!" I shout as a shot of lightning hits the stage and burns a hole in the gym floor. Students start to scream.

"It's okay!" Jocelyn tells everyone. "It doesn't understand us. Little guy, we're putting on a show. Please don't ruin it." The typhira shoots fire at Jocelyn's feet, and she jumps out of the way.

Fairy be! No one is moving. They don't realize these little things can't be reasoned with. They're going to tear the entire student body and the school apart. I look for Harlow. She's in the audience looking dazed, Cleo is swimming around in circles, and the other students are glued to their marks, watching everything unfold. It's as if the wish has made it impossible for them to worry about anything. And right now, they really should. I can try to save some, but I'm one person. I need help.

I look for Darlene, but she's nowhere to be seen. Then I spy her lamp wobbling on the stage floor. She saved herself… or so she thinks. A typhira spots the lamp and chucks it clear across the room. I need to go get that, but first I need to talk to Maxine. I physically might not be able to stop an army of mischievous, weather-changing creatures, but Wolfington and Professor Sebastian are right: Maxine can.

"Maxine!" I yell as I push AG out of the line of fire. I push other students in the same direction. "You have to stop the typhiras from destroying the school. Make your last wish!" I duck as a table comes flying at me.

"But…" Maxine hesitates, looking out at her family huddling together in a corner. "I haven't had a chance to perform yet." A table goes flying across the room and hits the front of the mermaid tank. A small fissure starts to spread. We cannot let that tank burst.

I start crawling toward Maxine as things fly around her. The typhiras are everywhere now. Hanging from the curtains, chewing through the rafters, and forming a hole in the ceiling. Rain is dripping down onto AG and Jax's heads. They stare up at it in wonder.

"The rain is so pretty," I hear Jocelyn say as she and Kayla sway back and forth singing their Enchantasia musical number. I dive at them and push them into the corner with the others.

"I know you want to be a star, but you already are one," I reason. "You gave everyone a chance to forget about the real world for a bit, but now it's time to bring them back, before someone gets hurt. If that doesn't make you a star—the hero of this story—I don't know what does."

"But the musical will still go on," Maxine sniffs. "And I'll sound terrible."

"You'll sound like you," I rationalize. "And you'll still do a great job. You won't be alone!" I yell over the thunder. "I'll stand by your side the whole time." A bolt of lightning shoots above our head and lights the curtain on fire. "If there's still a gym left to have the show in."

A chandelier crashes into the tank. The mermaids passively watch it float to the bottom.

"Okay," Maxine says, taking a deep breath. "Let's make my last wish."

"You've got this." I grab her hand and walk her down

the stage steps to retrieve the lamp. Only it's no longer there. "Where's the lamp?" I panic.

"For the love of Grimm, it's up there!" Maxine points to the ceiling where a typhira is carrying the lamp in its teeth as it climbs toward the hole in the ceiling.

If it slips through there with the lamp, we could lose Darlene for good and never get to make that wish. "We have to get that…Maxine?" I look around. Where did she go?

I see her ascending one of the wall ladders that was used to hang the scenery. She never climbs ladders because her hands are too big for the rungs.

"What are you doing?" I yell.

"I have to save the lamp!" she shouts, as her family watches.

"You can do it, Maxine!" her mother encourages her.

That's all the motivation she needs because Maxine climbs higher. I hear Maxine's mother gasp as a typhira shoots a lightning bolt that hits inches from Maxine's feet. Another bolt blasts the ladder next to Maxine's hand engulfing it in flames. I hold my breath as several typhiras see what's going on and begin crawling in Maxine's direction. I have to help her.

"Too bad Maxine can't fly like me," Kayla says, and I do a double take.

A fairy with wings is standing next to me. "Kayla!" I shake her. "Can you carry me up to Maxine to help her?" Kayla looks at me strangely. "So that we can play a game and be happy?" "A game? Sure!" Her wings pop out of her bag and enlarge in size, and she offers me her hands.

I grab hold of them, and we lift off the ground, dodging lightning bolts from other typhiras as we fly. A typhira reaches out to knock Maxine off the ladder, and she loses her hold, hanging from one arm.

"Maxine!" her mother cries.

"Hang on!" I shout, and Maxine grabs hold just in time to see me and Kayla flying at her. I swing my legs with all my might and knock the typhira off the rung. "Take that, you little beastie!" I look at Maxine. "Keep going. You're almost there. I'll back you up."

Maxine nods, her tongue sticking out of her mouth as she concentrates on the climb. The typhira sits a few feet above her. It's holding the lamp, and from what I can tell, it's actually snickering. Don't get so cocky, buddy. Maxine is about to steal that lamp back from you!

She reaches up with her meaty hand, but the typhira knocks it away. She tries again, and the same thing happens. It's never going to let her get that lamp.

Swoosh! A lightning bolt comes way too close for comfort and almost sends Kayla and me spiraling to the ground. The smoke from the fires that started from the lightning is getting thicker and making it hard to see. I'm losing sight of Maxine.

"Fly up to that typhira," I instruct Kayla. "I have an idea." I look at Maxine. "Get ready to catch!" When we're eye-to-eye with the beast, I swing my legs, using as much momentum as I can muster.

"Gilly, watch out!" Maxine cries as the beast opens its mouth. I don't give it a chance to fire. I swing my leg around and catch its claw. The lamp gets knocked from its grasp. Yes! Maxine reaches out to grab it and misses. The lamp is falling! I look down and see a group of typhiras waiting to catch it before Kayla and I can get down there.

Whoosh! Blue flies in out of nowhere, and Maxine jumps on the carpet before I can even react. The carpet is flying down, down, down. Finally, Blue catches up and slides under the lamp in time for Maxine to grab it.

"Yes!" I shout as typhiras start climbing toward me and

Kayla in strikingly fast fashion. "Uh, Kayla, you should go!" She begins to fly toward Maxine as lightning strikes hit in quick succession. When we reach the ground, I run to Maxine, who is uncorking the lamp. "Good job, Blue," I tell the rug, petting it.

Darlene doesn't appear like she usually does, but finally, Maxine rubs the lamp, and she has no choice but to show up.

When Darlene fizzes out of the lamp, she looks miserable. "I know. You want your last wish."

"It doesn't mean you have to go," Maxine says. "You can stay here with me. Or I can give you to someone else at school. They can make wishes."

"I'm not sure that's a good idea," I say, moving as an umbrella goes flying by us.

"It's not," Darlene agrees, looking around. "I've made a mess of things here."

"You were a great wish-giver," Maxine counters. "And the musical is the most fun this school has had in forever. Maybe you should direct musicals in the genie world. I'm sure they'd love a musical as much as we do."

"That's true, dear," Darlene says, perking up. "Think of the genie story lines I could do." She stares into the smoky distance. "I see a boy, finding a lamp in a cave. He doesn't know it's magic, but he gets trapped and…"

"Darlene, write the musical later," I say as more chairs go up in flames. "Wish first!"

"Right," Darlene agrees. "Go for it, Maxine."

Maxine closes her eyes, hugs the lamp to her chest, and wishes. "I wish things at Fairy Tale Reform School could go back to the way they were before I made my first wish."

Darlene closes her eyes and mutters a few words. There's a gust of wind, a blast of sound, and *boom*! "Final wish granted," Darlene says.

We look around. The typhiras have vanished, but students everywhere are waking up, looking around as if they've been asleep for a thousand years.

"Hans Christian Anderson, why am I wearing pink?" I hear someone shout.

I smile. I never thought I'd say this, but thank the fairies, Professor Harlow is back!

CHAPTER 15

Make a Wish

There is a lot of confusion and yelling after that. Both Professor Harlow and Jocelyn refuse to do anything until they magically whip up their normal attire—head-to-toe black for Jocelyn and a dark purple for the former Evil Queen.

"That's much better," says Harlow, sighing deeply as she clips a black, satin cape around her neck and puts a glittery gold crown on her head. Her dark eyes narrow as she looks around the room, which is still smoking. Bright embers from put-out fires burn all around us. "Now, someone better start explaining what is going on, and fast."

"I don't understand what we're all doing in the gym," Rapunzel speaks up, looking around in horror at the overturned chairs and the curtains, which are still smoldering. The elf cleaning crew shows up and quickly puts the fires out. "We shouldn't be having a school musical and opening our doors to anyone with Rumpelstiltskin and Alva on the loose." She ticks off a list of grievances on her fingers. "No one has done a single background check, or set up a security station to collect weapons, or put up a cloaking spell on the school so we can't be attacked during the show." She pulls at her long hair absentmindedly. "Where is Pete and the Dwarf Police Squad anyway?"

I clear my throat. "I'm Pete. Sort of," I explain sheepishly. My professor's eyes are as big as saucers. "He's put me in charge while he's on vacation."

"He did what?" Flora thunders. "A child running the Dwarf Police Squad?"

"A former thief, no less," Harlow adds. "The rule is former villains cannot hold positions of power in law enforcement. Rapunzel, how could you allow this?"

"Me?" Rapunzel asks. "I didn't even know Pete was gone! How could he take a vacation with Alva on the loose? Where is the rest of the police squad?"

"The rest of the squad couldn't get here when the typhiras

showed up and messed up all the weather in the kingdom," I explain.

"There's no such thing as typhiras!" Blackbeard and Flora say at the same time.

"In fact, there *is* such a thing," Wolfington tells them. "We know because Professor Sebastian and I saw them. Sadly, we couldn't get anywhere near the gym due to the hallways and doors short-circuiting from all the lightning strikes they made."

Beauty runs into the room, and AG rushes into her arms. "I couldn't get down the halls. The doorways aren't working," she says. "Is everyone okay? I heard the bridge was flooded to the castle, and no one can get here."

"We made it by boat," Maxine's father pipes up.

"Who are you?" Harlow snaps. "Why is there a large family of ogres listening to private school matters?"

"And why are we even *having* a musical?" Headmistress Flora is aghast. "Did I approve this? Why do I not remember approving a musical with all the other concerns the school has going on at the moment?"

"And who put me in pink? Such a ghastly color," Harlow adds.

"Agreed!" Jocelyn whines. "Why do I keep hearing the

same song in my head, over and over and over again, driving me insane? It's so happy." Others mumble in agreement.

"Why are AG and I dressed like we're going to a ball?" Jax asks.

"I hate performing," AG tells us. "Are you telling me I was about to go on stage? Because no, just no!"

"I don't even remember writing a musical!" Madame Cleo scratches her chin, her pale-blue tail swishing back and forth.

"I suspect a curse!" Rapunzel says, and everyone starts to agree. "How else do you explain this unusual series of events?"

Maxine slowly raises her hand. "It's not so unusual if you have a magic lamp."

Maxine's mom's jaw drops. Her drool puddles onto the floor. "Maxine, you didn't!"

Maxine won't look at her. Instead, she grabs the lamp in question, which is corked closed and opens it. Darlene oozes out.

"Maxine, our deal is done!" says Darlene, who has a tissue in her hand and looks as if she's been crying. "Genies don't come back to visit or miss their masters—we have thousands of them during our job run—so I really am not even supposed to be here right now at a—WAAAH!" She blows her nose.

"You made a wish with a genie?" Harlow thunders. "Of all the foolish moves a student could—"

"*Harlow*, please let me handle this." Headmistress Flora clears her throat. "Now, Maxine, I can understand the appeal of making a wish with Miss, uh…?"

"Darlene," the genie supplies, bowing to Flora. "Genie services for the past four thousand years. Give or take a few." She winks at us. "But I don't look a day over a thousand, do I?" She laughs, but Harlow looks as if she might breathe fire.

"It's nice to meet you, Miss Darlene," says Flora. "I assume you gave our Maxine three wishes?" Darlene nods. "What were they?"

Darlene looks at Maxine. "It's sort of complicated."

"What were they?" Harlow shrieks.

"I wished for everyone at school to be happy." Maxine hangs her head sadly.

"Oh." Flora looks surprised and glances at the other professors as the elf cleaning crew starts mopping around us and spraying ELF Cleaning Spray. "Why did you think we were unhappy?"

"Because all anyone here thinks about anymore is villains!" Maxine cries. "For a school supposedly teaching us how to be good in the fairy tale world, we spend a lot of time worrying about villains. What happened to regular school stuff? Homework? Our magical fairy pets and spending time with our friends?" Her shoulders sag. "It's like there's no time for that anymore. All anyone wants to do is talk about stopping someone who hasn't even shown up yet. We're just kids, but I don't feel like one with all this stuff going on."

The room is unusually quiet. Flora looks heartbroken while Harlow shuffles nervously. Wolfington pulls on his beard, but Professor Sebastian grabs Beauty's hand and smiles proudly at Maxine. What she says actually makes some sense.

"I know my wish didn't turn out as planned, but I did manage to make people smile and think about something other than war for a change." Maxine looks at all of us. "There's still so much good and beauty at Fairy Tale Reform School. I just wanted everyone to see that."

Professor Sebastian smiles at Maxine. "I think we owe these students an apology," he says to his fellow professors. "Maxine has brought up a good point."

"She has?" Rapunzel and Harlow say at the same time.

"Yes," Flora agrees. "We've lost sight of what's important at this school—and that's teaching our students how to thrive in the face of adversity. Not live in fear. If we stop living our lives, then Rumpelstiltskin and Alva have already won."

"But we must be ready," Harlow insists.

"And we will be," Flora continues. "But we should make time for fun too."

"You're right." Rapunzel plops down on a chair. "Planning battles all the time is exhausting. I don't know how you villains do it, plotting and thieving all the time."

"*Former* villains," Wolfington reminds her, and Blackbeard burps. "I'm curious, Maxine: What were your other two wishes?"

Maxine looks at her feet. "The second was to have a good voice, so I could get the lead in the school musical."

"Which I don't remember writing!" Madame Cleo sounds aghast.

"Why would you do that?" Jack asks as he tries to pry himself out of his formfitting beanstalk costume.

Maxine shrugs. "My voice is terrible, and I really wanted people to like me, I guess."

"Maxine, we already like you," AG tells her.

"You don't have to have the lead or a great voice for us to want to be around you," Jax agrees.

"We're your friends no matter what," Kayla reminds her.

"Besides, we already know you're tone-deaf," Jocelyn says. I shoot her a look.

"And as much as you want us to be happy, we want *you* to be happy too," I add.

"I love you guys," Maxine says, eyes glistening. "Let's hug!"

We gather round to hug her, and I hear Maxine's mom say, "She's a lucky girl to have friends like that. Good singing voice or not."

Darlene dabs at her eyes. "This really is the loveliest group of children I've ever met."

"Isn't it?" Flora agrees.

"So then, I take it the third wish was to correct the first wish?" Rapunzel asks.

Maxine nods sadly. "I didn't want to. Darlene didn't want to either."

"I just wanted to direct the musical before I left!" Darlene argues. "The children were so good! Especially Mr. Jax. Such a strong speaking voice."

"Really?" Jax stands straighter and clears his throat. "I mean, I guess I do speak well." His voice is suddenly deeper. Rapunzel rolls her eyes.

"But now we'll never have the chance," Maxine says sadly. "The typhiras showed up before showtime because of my wishing—I've always wanted to see one—and when they arrived, they were tearing the gym apart! Gilly knew someone would get hurt. She'd been warning me since I made my wishes that everyone walking around in a happy fog could be dangerous if we were attacked, but I wouldn't listen." Maxine squeezes my hand. "But Gilly reminded me that keeping the school and my friends safe was more important than any musical."

"I just did what any friend would do," I say. "I didn't want anyone to get hurt, but I couldn't stop the typhiras on my own. A third wish, however, could."

"Miss Cobbler convinced you to give up your third wish to save the school?" Harlow looks at me curiously. "Interesting."

"What is it, Harlow?" Flora asks.

"I find it intriguing that a reformed thief would have the power to convince someone with a wish to make things right," Harlow says. "Only a very clever girl who cares about the greater good could do that."

"Someone like that would make a fine police chief one day, don't you think?" Professor Sebastian has a twinkle in his eye.

Rapunzel and Flora look at one another. "Why yes, I think she would," Rapunzel agrees. "Looks like the royal court might have to reexamine some of our rules about who can and can't lead us in Enchantasia, especially where the police are concerned."

"Really?" I smile big and wide. "Yes!" I shout.

"That doesn't mean you have the job yet," Professor Sebastian reminds me.

"I know, sir." But I still can't help but smile. Knowing that a lowly reformed thief like me has the ability to change the minds of the royal court gives me hope.

"Well, I should probably get back to my lamp now," Darlene says.

"I'll take a wish!" A troll in the back rushes forward to grab the lamp.

A fairy flies forward. "Me too!"

Maxine, Harlow, and I block the lamp.

"No more wishes will be conducted here," Harlow tells them.

I pick up Darlene's lamp. "I think I know just the person to hide Darlene's lamp far, far away till she's ready for a new master."

"Good idea," Darlene says. "I'd love some time off to do some directing in the genie world. A good long rest would allow me to do that."

I run the lamp over to Madame Cleo's tank, hand it to Blackbeard, and whisper a favor. "Could someone take this to our friend Hayley? I'm sure she can find a safe spot to place Darlene."

Hayley is part mermaid, so I'm sure she'll find a good current and send Darlene on a voyage to far-off shores. That will keep her out of anyone's hands—or villains' clutches.

"Aye, aye, Miss Gillian." Blackbeard climbs a ladder on the side of the tank to bring it up to Madame Cleo.

"Goodbye, Maxine!" Darlene waves as she floats behind Blackbeard. "Till we meet again, my friend! Remember, wear red lipstick when you're going out, and always act like the star you are!"

"Goodbye, Darlene!" Maxine says. "Thank you for everything!"

We wave as she seeps back into her lamp and disappears from sight.

"Kayla!"

Kayla's mom runs into the gym clutching the fairy book, and I instantly freeze.

"There you are," Angelina says, giving her daughter a hug. "When I heard the thunder and saw the lightning around the school, I feared the worst." She looks at the rest of us with trepidation. "The book is finished. I know how this all ends."

"And?" Flora holds her breath.

"I…am not sure." Angelina looks at the kids standing around us and tries to smile, but I can tell she's worried.

"That's because the future isn't written yet," Wolfington reminds her. "The future can always be changed."

"Very true," Professor Sebastian agrees.

I stare at the book hungrily. Now I want to know what's written in that book. What Rumpelstiltskin has planned. Whether Anna is involved in it. What all this means for Enchantasia. And what we can do to stop it or change it. But Angelina isn't talking, and my teachers aren't asking. Instead, most of them are smiling and whispering.

"Whatever is written can wait to be read until later this evening, don't you agree, Angelina?" Flora asks.

"Yes," Angelina agrees. "Nothing is going to happen

today. Or the next, or the day after that, or even the day after that, or…"

"My point is, we have time," Flora tells everyone. "And I think what we need most right now, especially after all this wish making, and a typhira attack, and learning the little buggers are actually real…"

"And they flung goo all over our radishes and strawberry crops," I add. "There's none left in the kingdom."

"They did?" Harlow asks. "That's impossible! From what I've read about typhira legend, they don't make slime. They shoot lightning bolts. Besides, they're allergic to eating anything that grows in the earth."

"Sounds unhealthy," Ollie comments.

I'm so confused. If they're allergic to radishes and strawberries, then they wouldn't go near the radishes. "But…"

"But what?" Jax prods.

This makes no sense, I want to say. But then that would lead to a big story about everything he's missed while he's been under the enchantment. So instead, I say, "I'll tell you later."

Jax grins. "Deal."

"As I was saying," Flora interrupts. "I think what we need right now is a little entertainment." She looks at Maxine.

"And perhaps a song from this musical that Madame Cleo and Harlow wrote."

"Fairy be," I hear Harlow mumble, as Madame Cleo says, "How delightful! Yes!"

"But no one remembers it," Kayla tells her.

"I think one person does." Flora looks hard at Maxine. "And I'm sure her family would like to hear her sing."

"Me?" Maxine begins to back away. "But my voice. I told you, I'm terrible."

"I'm sure you're not terrible," Flora says kindly. "Even if you are off-key, who cares? You're among family and friends." Everyone nods, but Maxine still looks hesitant. "Please? To make up for all this…mischief that's occurred?"

"Okay," Maxine agrees, looking bashful, yet excited at the same time. Her parents gather round as do the other students as the elf cleaning crew continues to clean up in the background. "I'll sing the opening number, 'Oh, Enchantasia.' It goes like this: 'Oh, Enchantasia! The land we call our own!'"

Maxine's voice warbles, cracks, and almost shatters the glasses on the nearby table, but it doesn't matter. She's happy. We're happy. And we're laughing and cheering her on.

Because for the moment, everything at Fairy Tale Reform School is just as it should be: unpredictable.

Pegasus Postal Service

Flying Letters Since the Troll War!

FROM: Mrs. Cobbler (2 Boot Way)

TO: Gilly Cobbler (Fairy Tale Reform School)

FOR YOUR EYES ONLY!

Gillian,

I'm sorry it's taken so long for me to write you this note. Things in the village have been so hectic with Pete gone. And with the radish and strawberry shortage, I couldn't make Father's beloved rhubarb-strawberry pie. In any case, Pete's back now and not a moment too soon!

You asked about your grandmother Pearl, and I think it's time I tell you everything, including where she came from. She's a real spitfire! Tangoed with several villains in her day. Had that fairy spirit in her, even if she was only half fairy. Did I ever tell you that? Father didn't want me to, but I was so proud. You, my darling, are part fairy. And

---

with the way things are going in Enchantasia these days, I have a feeling having fairy blood running through your veins is going to come in handy.

But don't take my word for it. Ask Grandma Pearl yourself! I've already sent her a post saying you'll come calling on her soon. I've tucked her address in here. She's a bit sheltered these days and very private, but she will want to see you. She hasn't laid eyes on you since she gave you a blessing and a gift as a baby. You were the only one of my children she bestowed one on before...well, I'll let her tell you the rest.

All my love,
Mother

WELCOME TO ROYAL ACADEMY!

From the desk of the Fairy Godmother*

Headmistress Olivina would like to cordially welcome* you to Royal Academy for your first year of ruler training!

Please arrive with a training wand, a mini magical scroll, several quills, and no fewer than three pairs of dress shoes. (Please note: glass slippers should have scuffed soles to prevent injuries due to heavily waxed floors.)

Personal stylists and tailors will be on-site to assist all students in creating their signature royal style. We look forward to seeing you one week from today!

◇◇◇◇◇◇◇◇

*The word welcome *is only a formality! Attendance at RA is* mandatory *for all young royals in the kingdom. Questions should be sent by magical scroll to the Fairy Godmother's office.*

Dan Mandel, I'm so lucky to call you both my agent and my friend. Thank you for always being in my corner.

It truly takes a village when writing a book, and I'm so thankful to have such an amazing support group, including wonderful writer friends Elizabeth Eulberg, Kieran Scott, Tiffany Schmidt, Courtney Sheinmel, Katie Sise, and Jennifer E. Smith, as well as mom friends who help me with school pickups and activities when I'm traveling for work, including Elpida Agenziano, Joanie Cook, Lisa Gagliano, AnnMarie Gagliano, Christi Lennon, Maria Small, Melissa McCabe, Jeannine Megias, and Kristen Marino.

Acknowledgments

If Darlene the Magic Genie gave me three wishes, my first would be to always work with editor Kate Prosswimmer. Kate, you are the most wonderful editor and partner and are always up for an adventure with the Fairy Tale Reform School kids. I'm also thankful for the entire Sourcebooks team, including Steve Geck, Stefani Sloma, Beth Oleniczak, Margaret Coffee, Stephanie Graham, Nicole Hower, Todd Stocke, and Dominique Raccah for all the love they've given this series. Cassie Gutman, thank you for making sure I dot all my i's and cross my t's and for making sure everything sounds just right! To Mike Heath for another incredible cover design. I don't know how you do it, but each cover is even more spectacular than the last!

JEN CALONITA'S BRAND-NEW SERIES

ROYAL ACADEMY REBELS

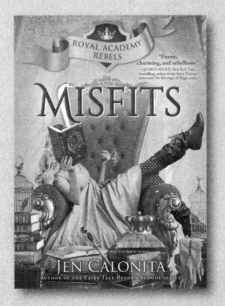

NOT EVERYONE BORN ROYAL IS MEANT TO RULE

Read on for a sneak peek of Misfits.

Chapter 1

Once There Was a Girl...

꙳

"Hold still. I just want to help you." I keep my voice calm yet firm. If she moves too quickly, she could do more damage. I need to be careful not to spook her.

"That's a good girl," I coo, taking a step closer. "Stay right where you are. You're safe now."

Crack! My bare foot snaps a twig, startling her. She hobbles farther into the brush, making it hard for me to see anything but her panicked eyes. If she moves any deeper into the branches, I won't be able to reach her.

"It's okay," I tell her as some of our friends quietly gather around to watch me work.

I step deeper into the thicket, the chittering of the insects intensifying in the shady trees that surround me. The air is hot, and I'm sweating despite having left my jacket and skirt back in the clearing. I snag a vine from above me and use it to tie back my pale-blond locks. She's watching with interest as I fix my hair.

"I'm not going to hurt you," I promise, my voice barely more than a whisper. Slowly, I pull something from my pocket I know she'll like. I place the handful of cashews I swiped from last night's dinner on a branch between us. She eyes the nuts for a moment, then quickly eats one. Nice!

As she crunches on the nuts, I stay very still, listening for any sounds. I hear an owl hoot in the distance and water babbling in a nearby brook, but for the most part, the forest is unusually quiet.

"Good snack, right?" I ask, trying to make her feel at ease. "I know I look young, but I have a lot of experience doing what I'm doing, so don't be nervous."

She tilts her head at me.

"It's true! Just last week, Nox came to see me for a sore throat, and I mixed him a tonic that cleared it right up. And when Peter lost his sense of smell after having a bad cold, I made a broth that fixed everything." I inch closer to the tangle of brambles where she's perched. She doesn't move, so

I keep talking. "And when Deirdre sprained her ankle after running from a bear in the Hollow Woods, I made her a splint, and now she's walking just fine."

I hold out my hand. She doesn't recoil, but she doesn't move any closer either. Time to bring out the big guns. I strain my neck toward my friends below me. "Deirdre? Can you please back me up here?"

Deirdre takes a flying leap, landing on the tree branch next to me.

Did I mention she's a flying squirrel?

Or that the "she" I'm trying to help is a songbird?

Lily, my bearded dragon, pokes her head out of my shirt pocket to listen to Deirdre's mix of clicks, clucks, and high-pitched squeaks that will hopefully get through to the little red bird with the injured wing. I can only make out parts of what she's saying.

I'm not fluent in squirrel yet.

Not like other humans! Really cares... Knows medicine! She can help... Trust her. We do! Friend!

I smile at that last word. I don't have many friends. When you tell the kids in the schoolyard you can talk to animals, most call you a liar. Or a freak. Some even say you're evil.

Hey, I get it. It's an unusual, uh, *talent* to have, but it's a big part of who I am. Besides, I am really good at this "helping animals" thing.

I notice her wing is sagging. She might have snagged it taking off from a tree, or maybe she bumped into a giant. My animal friends say it happens a lot. The songbird curiously sniffs my fingers with her beak.

"That's it now. Climb in," I say in a soft voice. Deirdre chimes in too, squeaking her encouragement.

Finally, after a moment of hesitation, the bird steps into my steady palm! Below, I hear the chattering cheer of my friends.

"What's your name?" I ask the little bird as I carefully cradle her fragile body.

She chirps in a small singsong voice.

"Scarlet? How lovely to meet you, Scarlet." I stand up and walk her over to my office.

My office is really just a quilt I stole from the maid's quarters. (Mother wanted it tossed anyway.) On the blanket, I have my satchel of herbs that I pinched from the kitchen and mending tools I've gathered from our sewing kits. I store everything in a hollow log near the clearing so no one questions what I'm up to when I go on my "daily walks" beyond our garden gates.

I rinse my hands with the little jug of water I've brought with me, then open my satchel and pull out the small fabric slings I've been making while Mother thought I was practicing my needlepoint. Finding one that looks to be the right size, I get to work, setting the bird's wing as best I can. Scarlet tweets excitedly when I'm finished. Then I mix basil, chamomile, and willow bark seeds together with the water.

"This should help with the pain," I tell her. "Come see me again in a few days, and we'll see how your wing is mending. If you want, we can help you find a safe place to sleep in the meantime." I place the mixture in a tiny thimble and encourage Scarlet to drink. After a few sips, she tweets at me excitedly, and I know she's saying "thank you." She has a sibling that lives in a hollowed-out old oak three trees over so she'll be safe there while she heals. That's a relief.

Everyone is so excited about Scarlet's new sling that they can't keep quiet. Between the neighs, snorts, and chittering from other animals, I'm worried a big, bad wolf—or worse, the main house—will wonder what's going on.

"Keep it down!" I say with a laugh. "You're going to give

us away!" The noise decreases slightly, and I lean back and soak in the sunlight filtering through the trees.

I live for moments like this. Being a creature caretaker is all I've wanted to be. Mother thought it was a phase I'd grow out of, which is why she didn't pay Father any mind when he bought me a leather satchel filled with "animal doctor" supplies. But ever since, I've been pulling spiders out of drinking jugs, mending birds' wings on my bedroom windowsill, rescuing wayward kittens from hungry foxes, and getting an occasional visit from a unicorn that has lost its sense of direction.

I won't be *growing out of it* anytime soon. I don't know how I'm able to talk to animals or know what they need, but I'm smart enough to know you don't give up a gift like that. I hope that someday even creatures beyond Cobblestone Creek will seek me out for help. But first, I need to find someone to teach me proper creature care techniques.

"*Devinaria!*"

I sit up straight. The birds stop chirping. Lily pokes her head out of my pocket again, and we stare at each other worriedly. No one should be looking for me out here. Not when I swore I was going to Mother Hubbard's Tea Shoppe with some girls from class.

"Devinaria! Where are you?"

Drooping dragons! The voice grows louder, and I hear trumpets sounding in the distance. It's as if a royal procession is about to roll right through the forest. I hear footsteps, then heavy breathing, as if someone's running in our direction.

I jump up, trying to put all my supplies away before someone sees them. Then I remember what I'm wearing. I look down at my undergarments and torn shirt and spin around in a desperate search for my skirt. The shirt and bloomers I'm wearing aren't much different from the outfits the boys in the village wear, but the ensemble is definitely not—as my mother would say—"princess appropriate."

"Princess Devinaria!" Our footman Jacques sounds out of breath as he stumbles into the clearing. "There you are!"

I cringe. I *hate* when people call me that. "Devin is just fine, Jacques." I try to maintain an air of dignity as I grab my skirt from a bush and quickly wrap it around my waist, pinning it on the side where I've cut it for easy on-and-off situations. With a ribbon tied and draped down the side, no one can tell I sliced the skirt open (other than Jacques, who has just seen my little trick and looks quite alarmed).

"How, um, did you even find me out here?" I run a hand through my hair and pull out a leaf. "Did you need something?" I ask him.

"Miss, it's urgent!" Jacques's eyes widen as the trumpets sound closer. "Your mother...father...the trumpets... Miss, *it's* coming, and..."

I inhale sharply and stumble backward. Lily flicks her tongue wildly. "No," I whisper.

"Yes!" Jacques insists, grabbing my hand. "Your invitation is here!"

About the Author

Jen Calonita is the author of the Fairy Tale Reform School series, the Royal Academy Rebels series, and other books like *Secrets of My Hollywood Life* and *Turn It Up*. She rules Long Island, New York, with her husband, Mike; princes, Tyler and Dylan; and their Chihuahuas, Captain Jack Sparrow and Ben Kenobi. The only castle she'd ever want to live in is Cinderella's at Walt Disney World. She'd love for you to visit her at jencalonitaonline.com and on Twitter @jencalonita.